SISTERS IN SIN

PRIMULA BOND

mischief

Mischief
An imprint of HarperCollins*Publishers*
77–85 Fulham Palace Road,
Hammersmith, London W6 8JB

www.mischiefbooks.com

A Paperback Original 2013

First published in Great Britain in ebook format by
HarperCollins*Publishers* 2012

Copyright © Primula Bond 2012

Primula Bond asserts the moral right to
be identified as the author of this work

A catalogue record for this book is
available from the British Library

ISBN-13: 9780007534807

Set in Sabon by FMG using Atomik ePublisher from Easypress

Find out more about HarperCollins and the environment at
www.harpercollins.co.uk/green

CONTENTS

Contents

Chapter One

In my rush to get away from him I'd become totally lost. My brand-new boots pinched horribly as I slipped and scurried across the wet worn flagstones, under green flaking arches, along narrow alleyways, beside stagnant canals, and finally into a little square where I stopped to catch my breath.

I glanced round. The rain had found its way into the square after me, but not the strange man. There was no one to be seen. Ridiculously, I almost wished that I'd stopped being so paranoid and just asked him what he wanted. That's what happens when you spend too much time on your own. Maybe this trip wasn't such a good idea after all. Not right. Not healthy. And just then I would have preferred to be with anyone, even a weirdo, rather than, like now, totally alone.

I took out my mobile. A call to Hazel, my mate and business partner who was holding the fort back in London, should sort me out. She was the one who'd told me to fuck off and get out of her face. In the most caring kind of way.

'How's it going?' I could tell Hazel was busy, and distracted. Probably a client was standing by the counter as she talked, waiting to pay. In the background, red buses rumbling by. The pedestrian crossing beeping just outside our shop. 'Found any good outlets yet?'

'Some. Most of the glass shops are very quiet this time of year. And their stuff is so – quaint. Not sure our super-contemporary clients want fussy little seashells and conches scattered all over their minimalist interiors.'

'Well, think outside the box and find something cutting-edge, then. Been out to the workshops on Murano yet?'

'Give me a chance! I've only been here two days!'

'Two more to go, then. So you'd better get your skates on, girl. And there's no need to be petulant with me. We've got to justify sending you over there on expenses. So. What about your leisure time? Any nice men to take your mind off things? It's the most romantic city on earth, after all.'

'Yeah. Rub it in, why don't you. Especially with Valentine's Day just around the corner and everyone getting ready for Carnivale with their masks and costumes

2

and all. I must be the only person here without a lover.' I thumped my backside down on the rim of an old well in the middle of the square. A pigeon came up, tilted its head and pecked experimentally at my toe. 'And to top it all I've got a stalker.'

Hazel cackled. 'You wish!'

'Seriously. Everywhere I go, every shop, every corner, he's there.' The well was damp, and so now was my bottom. 'Watching me.'

'If you say so, doll. What does he look like?'

'Like a stalker! You know, tall, long dark coat, some kind of brimmed hat, a fedora thing – I haven't seen his face, but it's like he's this shadow, sliding over the walls behind me, following me everywhere.'

'Sounds like the kinky fantasy of a frustrated old mare to me.'

'It's true. He exists!' I protested, laughing nevertheless. 'I first saw him passing down the Grand Canal on a *vaporetto* not long after I got here. Then coming out of Harry's Bar last night. He was even outside my hotel this morning. But it's funny you should use the word "kinky" ...'

As always she'd hit the nail on the head. Inside the head, even. She knew the way my mind worked, how it basically revolves around sex or the lack of it. We were bosom mates – no, not *that* kind of bosom. Neither of us are – were – that way inclined. But she just knew me

3

so well after hours, nights, weekends, years of talking long into the night about our life and loves. She knew how splitting up with my latest married man was inevitable. They always went back to their wives. But to top it all I was pushing forty, my faithful stock of fuck buddies had also run out and she certainly wasn't prepared to lend me her precious Tony.

So, yes, I had fantasised about the scary stalker.

More than that, I'd actually slowed down deliberately coming out of Harry's Bar last night, wondering if he might turn and follow me back to the Danieli Hotel. I picked my way over the bridge and along the wide promenade that ran from the bar along the outer edge of Piazza San Marco, trying not to get my feet wet in the remaining puddles from the rain and the *acqua alta* that had flooded over the piazza at high tide. I let my long red cashmere scarf trail behind me like bait as the cold breeze blew off the black lagoon and whipped my hair across my eyes. But when I looked back he wasn't there.

At the hotel I wandered across the large tiled hallway and into the warm piano bar humming with people, the sweet smell of cocktails and the saccharine melodies being picked out by an ancient pianist. I took the cocktail that the mustachioed barman flourished at me. I'd never travelled on my own before, and on my first night I'd automatically scanned the place for talent as if I was still cruising the bars in London, painted on my best smile, hitched up my tits in my best push-up bra, crossed my legs provocatively, Sharon Stone-style. Realised there was nothing doing. I was being comprehensively ignored. And when I realised that the manager was observing me from the doorway, wondering if I was a hooker, I shrugged at him, jangled my room key ostentatiously and went up to bed.

But something had definitely come over me since then. In the two days I'd been in Venice a kind of charmed fatigue was creeping into my bones along with the damp air of the city. I couldn't be bothered to toy with what was in front of me, the jostling crowds, proposing couples, even random barmen or winking Italians. I wanted the imaginary, the impossible, something ephemeral that I was sure was waiting just out of sight.

That second night I hung around in the bar for at least another hour. Something about the very fact that I was ignoring them seemed to invite smiles from various guys, all trying to catch my eye over the narrow, tailored shoulders of their haughty dates. But I just sat up high on a bar stool so that the stalker could see me clearly above the potted palms if he came in.

And when he didn't come in I realised how pathetic I was being. Of course he wasn't coming in. He probably didn't exist! But still I ascended the grand curving staircase instead of taking the lift, in case he came gliding in through the front door. Then I kicked shut the door and fell backwards across the big ornate bed, my dress up round my fanny, listening as the traffic, both human and watery, ebbed and flowed in the cold night outside my window.

I couldn't get him out of my head. I imagined him opening the door without ceremony and without a word, walking soundlessly over to where I'm lying, leaning over me, still wearing that long dark coat, the hat still shadowing his face.

I sit up on my elbows and try to see what he looks like. Various faces flit across my imagination. My ex-boyfriend. My university tutor. Hazel's Tony. The barman. But all I can see is white skin and a pointed chin, and a mouth set in a grim line. He reaches out a gloved hand and lifts my dress right up, over my waxed snatch, and of course he sees I'm not wearing any knickers. He holds the dress up for a long moment while his other hand moves deliberately and thoroughly over his crotch, rubbing it almost thoughtfully as he stares at my body. Then he lets the dress flutter down again high up over my stomach, leaving my pussy bare.

Now he leans over me and pushes my thighs open. His gloves are of some kind of expensive leather but still they snag slightly on my skin. One long finger strokes towards where the pussy lips swell on either side of the neat line of topiary, but stops short of touching them, which only makes them pulse all the more. He pushes my legs wider still, and still I can't see his face, but I can see a seam of moisture between his lips and the serrated tips of his white teeth.

My face is on a level with his crotch, and through his open coat I see the bulge in his black trousers, the big outline of his cock, thick and hard and incongruous against the thin, mean body. I stretch my hand out tentatively towards it, wondering if he'll slap it back, but he is almost like a statue now, holding my legs open, staring down at me, his eyes invisible, his cheeks and chin incredibly white and smooth, no sign of any bristles. I touch that hard outline, and all he does is tip his head very slightly back and swallow. So I start to unzip his trousers, no reaction, get my hand inside his flies, still as stone, I pause again to see if he'll stop me, then as soon as I touch the smooth surface of his cock I'm horny as hell, never mind what he's feeling.

At last there's the faintest crackle in his throat, and that flicks the switch for me. I love a man at my mercy. I grip him harder, but suddenly he lifts his hands from my legs and grabs either side of my head, covering my ears so that all I can hear is the thump of my heart and the rush of my breath and the slight creak of his leather gloves.

He shoves my head into his groin. I expect to smell sweat and the salty hint of spunk but there is only the tang of strong soap. He grinds my face harder against him so that my nose squashes up against his thick curly hair and his jutting cock. As I pull slightly away his penis jumps at my face, banging against my nose. There is nothing but the soapy darkness, the rub of the thick fabric of his trousers and coat, and the almost rigid cock poking me. The stalker's hands are really tight over my head, smothering my face inside his trousers so I can hardly breathe. I open my mouth to get air, and my tongue slicks across the tip of his cock. It swells bigger and harder in response, and yes now there's a droplet of moisture there on the tip as I take a tentative lick, smearing it across my chin as his cock slips away from me. I lick again, think of it as my lollipop. It jumps again, he pulls back but only for a second, he jerks urgently at my mouth, losing control, aiming it like a weapon. So his knob slips stickily into my mouth.

My pussy twitches with the thrill, the menace and the sheer excitement of causing an erection in such a cold, stony figure. I can't relish it properly because I'm sprawled awkwardly on my front now, towards the edge of the high bed. I can't move because I'm holding on to the stalker's coat and then his skinny hips to balance, so all I can do is rub myself against the duvet. He thrusts himself hard against me, almost breaking my teeth as he forces his cock further inside my mouth. I think I can hear a muttered curse, but it's only a whisper. I follow the motion of his body with my mouth, trying hard not to bite him.

I grip the top of his legs and keep the rounded knob of his enormous cock firmly in my mouth. The whole shaft presses against my tongue, rubs against my teeth. I open my jaw wider. He's huge now. I push the rigid length away from my throat with my tongue. Every move makes him stiffer. I start to suck and I can taste him, clean skin mixed with the sweet salt trickling through the slit. Funny how even an automaton like him won't be able to control his own spunk. His hands grip harder on my head, but he is moving more now. I can hear a low moan as he thrusts his cock against the roof of my mouth, filling it. My tongue traces the veins on its surface. My mouth moves up and down and I nip the taut flesh. He pushes in hard, pushing it right down my throat, spreading his thighs a little wider and tipping his pelvis to get a better angle, and now there's another faint scent which seems released from his clothes, a smoky musky aroma that seems to curl up through my nostrils right into my head. It's pleasant, clean, sensual even, but I can't place it.

I move to keep a grip on him and my pussy opens against the old-fashioned brocade of the bed cover and it scrapes the tender clit hiding inside and it's my turn to flinch with pleasure and groan. But that seems to displease him. His hands imprison my cheeks and force my head to rock back and forth some more, my teeth and lips sliding right away from his long cock before he slams my face forwards again. His cock is deep down my throat, but I'm good at this. I'm known for it. And the reason I'm always up for it, enjoy it so much, feeling that shaft of excited male muscle in my mouth, gagging me to choking point, is that I can imagine it doing the same inside me. Soon it will be fucking me.

Somehow I know that's not going to happen tonight. This man has come to me for his pleasure, not mine, so as I suck harder and faster and move my mouth up and down I move my body in time, rubbing my pussy up, down, on the brocade, rough embroidery scraping on my clit, making it burn, making my pussy twitch and clench furiously, furious I suppose with him, too, but as my stalker starts to buck against me, I feel the little rush of orgasm just on the edge of me, not really far enough inside, and as it blooms out of me I feel the thick gush of his spunk gathering in my mouth, spurting down my tongue, and I swallow it, determined to show him that he's picked the right girl for a blow job, how the hell did he know, is it my luscious lips, always painted a dark red and fashioned exactly for sucking on something sweet? I swallow it all, the familiar slight reflux in my throat making me nip at him so that he jerks backwards but it's still spurting out and he stays rammed inside my mouth, my face jammed between his hands, until he's done.

I let the cock slide out of my mouth, and turn quickly

on to my knees like a doggy, offering my backside up to him for another go, and panting eagerly as I smile back at him over my shoulder, running my tongue over my lips in invitation.

But he shakes his head, dipping the hat over his eyes, then pushes me roughly so that I fall forwards on to the bed. He sneers, but he hasn't said a word. I haven't noticed him zipping himself up, but he flicks his coat closed and as he swishes away from me again there's that scent released into the air, catching in my throat. I can only describe it as spiritual. Candles. Incense. A church smell. Then he strides across the carpet and leaves through the still open door.

'Say what?' Far away in Long Acre, Hazel sighed.

'What you said about the fantasy – oh, never mind.' I could hear the other line ringing in the shop.

'Whatever. You've been watching too many movies, Jen. Now get a grip, buy some Venetian glass at wholesale to keep us from going bust, and get your arse back here.'

I wasn't ready to let her go, but before I could keep her talking, maybe share the details of that particular fantasy, the phone went dead.

And then I heard it. Above my head. A moan, elongated as if someone was in pain, a sigh, then another moan. Impossible to ignore. The sound was brazen as it insinuated itself out of yet another Gothic window and ricocheted off the high surrounding walls. Sounds here always turn to echos: footsteps, church bells, the flapping of wings, the snap of a bed sheet. Atmospheric and intriguing, especially for a visiting stranger. But this was different. This was the private, human, sweaty whisper of sex. A creaking bed, headboard knocking on the wall. Oh God. Now I could see it. Them. In my mind. Strong male buttocks rearing up and thrusting in between eager, slender, gripping thighs.

I glanced round to see if anyone else was listening or coming out to shut them up, but the doors and windows in the little *campo* stared blankly back. They looked rusty and dusty, as if they hadn't been opened for years. Well, it was February, and foggy, and freezing cold. Only one was open, with a red curtain billowing out like a tongue over a box of geraniums.

I was imagining it. I started to stand up, but then a woman's voice murmured something, and her lover answered, his voice harsh with lust. Individual hairs started to rise on my neck, on the crown of my head, along my arms. The noises were excruciatingly intimate, making me blush, but they were also turning me on.

Now there was a creaking of bed springs and they started to sing slowly, in an unmistakable rhythm. I started to rub my hands up and down my thighs. It was time to go. But I was pinned to the spot by the noises. Also I had no idea where I was, or where I was going. The ragged moans rose, became closer together, stretched

12

into wordless gasping, sounding so close to fear or pain but we all know it's perfect pleasure, panting in time to the creaking bed. My nipples, already cold, stiffened instinctively, my silk camisole clinging to the hard points. I covered my ears, but moisture seeped into my knickers. How desperate did that make me, getting aroused by someone else's fucking? After my empty stalker fantasy, this was torture.

But the square was so silent. These were the only sounds. It was like I was in the room with them, seeing them through all the stages of whispering, kissing, touching, arousing each other in their bed right through to the fucking. I knew the man was inside her now, because every few seconds he gave a groan just like a tennis pro serving an ace, and that was what turned me on. The square reverberated with the rhythmic sounds, their animal groaning as the man's cock thrust again and again into the woman with those glorious two-tone moans. Why did nobody else hear? The bed was banging against the wall and they were almost shouting now, the moans rising to that uninhibited pitch where pleasure meets pain.

I realised I was rocking, too, on my damp seat, cold hands rubbing at myself under my coat, fingers creeping under my skirt to find my crotch, sliding inside my knickers, one finger matching the heady rhythm echoing from the window, running up, running down my crack, making it wet, making me jealous, I could picture the sex-soaked scene through that shuttered window, the rumpled sheets, the bed thumping against the wall, their mouths open, his cock pulling out, big and hard and glistening with her juice, her pussy pink and open and wet, then him slamming her back against the pillows as he thrust inside.

Like a wildlife film when you see lions humping. They were hard at it up there. My fingers rubbed faster across my crotch and then the woman was straining for breath, hissing, 'Yes, yes.' I vaguely thought, surely it should be '*si, si*'? Maybe she was riding him, breasts bouncing, hard nipples catching between his teeth, his fingers digging into her haunches to keep her rammed on to his big cock. Everything was rising to a crescendo. A ball of excitement rolled and tightened in my stomach as the creaking of the bed grew more violent. I moaned out loud as my own pussy sucked at my fingers and then I came, quickly and quietly, my knees weak as I shivered there on the stone well, cold and exhausted and even more frustrated than before.

Upstairs the groaning and panting stopped, regained a second momentum with a kind of desperate shriek, then died.

It was as if everyone was holding their breath, daring each other to be the first to move. Why does masturbating make you feel so alone? No one to hold or touch after, that's why. I got my own breath back and fumbled for my guidebook as if someone was watching me accusingly. Suddenly the door beneath the window opened. I pretended to study my map but glanced over the top of it to see what voluptuous, sated creature was emerging from the house.

But instead of a dishevelled Monica Bellucci lookalike in a fur coat and stilettos, with messed-up tendrils of black hair and scarlet lips, a slim, plain-looking figure with short fair hair in a long grey dress, thick tights and flat black lace-ups hurried out into the wintry light, fastening a billowing cape in a bow at her neck. Then, as she stepped backwards to call something up at the window she pulled a white cap and then a grey veil over her hair and fastened it with kirby grips. That woman *in flagrante* I'd been eavesdropping on, the afternoon adulteress, or whore, or honeymooning wife was actually – a nun!

I stifled a snort of laughter. Maybe she was in disguise. In fancy dress?

She put her hand up beside her mouth and called again. 'Carlo! Answer me!'

The man refused to come to the window. Some kind of row going on?

'For God's sake!'

Finally a man's hand pushed through the geraniums in the box and flung some cash down to the ground. Maybe she was a tom, after all?

'*Bastardo*! I don't want money!' the nun half hissed, half screamed, waving her arms out of the cape. 'I'm not one of your tourist groupies!'

Her accent was almost perfectly English, the smoker's sexy rasp totally at odds with the prim exterior.

'No?' He shouted down. 'Well, then you should start acting like a proper girlfriend and stay the night with me for once, instead of sneaking off after I've given you one. Oh, just fuck off back to your little prison before they notice you're missing.'

'Don't you dare! You know my situation there! You know I can't –'

I still couldn't see her face, but I could see that she was shaking. Her hands, raised in the air as if to try and reach up to him, smacked back down to her sides, the fingers furiously twisting and bunching up the thick material of the cloak.

'Well, I'm fed up with waiting. Plenty more where you came from.' He was at the window now. All I could see was a head of dark, curly hair and a navy sweater rolled up over big strong arms. His hands were curled into fists on the edge of the windowsill. A livid red scar ran round one wrist like a bracelet. 'Use the money to buy yourself a new prayer mat, or a Bible, or a nice fat candle, or whatever you use in there for kicks.'

'*Vaffanculo!*' she screeched, making the pigeon flap up in alarm. 'Go fuck yourself!'

16

She turned on her heel, threw the hood over her head, and rushed out through an archway on the far side of the square from where I'd entered. As I levered myself stiffly up from my damp seat, Carlo caught sight of me. His black eyes glittered furiously as if *I'd* done something wrong. Then he stopped, and looked right at where my coat was unbuttoned, my skirt still hoicked up round my thighs.

'You're all tarts!' At least I think that's what he said. Maybe it was 'Your last chance!' Either way I felt a rush of shame, followed by a rush of fury that he'd made me feel that way. He slammed closed the shutters and suddenly his window became as blind and deaf as all the others in this ethereal city.

I could hear her footsteps tapping away into the distance. Silence and darkness were gathering round me again, along with lanky tendrils of fog. I started to run after her. She was the only human being I'd seen in the last hour, after all. Not counting the stalker, who I reckoned wasn't human at all. Worse than that, I had no idea where I was and it wasn't funny any more. At least she'd be able to tell me the way back to my plush hotel on the Riva degli Schiavoni.

'*Scusi! Signorina!*' I called out, careering out from under the archway and on to a narrow, slippery pavement beside a sliver of green canal. There were no railings, and I nearly splashed straight into the water. As I fell back against the wall, heart juddering, I caught sight of a tall dark figure standing on the other side of the canal, framed by another archway. The hat shaded the face. All I could see was the high collar of his coat and the sharp chin turned sideways. In the dusk he was a whole lot spookier than in last night's fantasy. Downright scary. And he was, like me, intently watching the nun as she lifted one sturdy shoe to climb a little stone bridge.

As my voice echoed off the water she flinched and turned round sharply. Her ankle scooted out sideways, veering her towards the water. I gasped apologetically, but luckily instead of going into the canal she fell heavily against the stone balustrade of a little bridge.

'*Ach, cazzo!*'

'Oh, shit!'

We swore in unison, our voices amplified by the silent, slimy walls. I teetered carefully along the slippery stones, glancing again in the direction of the stalker. But by the time I had reached her and saw how awkwardly her ankle was twisted, the dark figure had vanished.

Chapter Two

'Hey, I'm sorry to startle you,' I stammered, kneeling down beside her as she groaned and rubbed her limp ankle. I checked again. Yes. He'd gone. 'I was only after some directions.'

Just as I wondered impatiently if she wasn't making a bit of a mountain out of a molehill with all this groaning and writhing, she looked up at me from under the cape, opened her mouth to reply, and there was a kind of punch inside my chest. She was like something out of a Botticelli painting. An angelic face staring out from a soft-focus tangle of other angelic faces in an advert for some perfume. There was no distant, starved, prematurely aged expression such as I would expect from a nun. Her pale heart-shaped face seemed to glow out of the shadow of the heavy material she was wearing, with high cheeks flushed so pink – from her recent secret fuck-fest, obviously – that they looked as if she was wearing blusher.

The tight grey frame of her veil accentuated that very absence of any make-up or artistry and in any case those huge blue eyes, long eyelashes and plump pink O of a mouth needed no mascara or lipstick, let alone the kind of invasive procedures involving needles that I'd been contemplating recently. She was ridiculously pretty; like a doll with life breathed into it.

'Help me!' she stuttered, glancing round anxiously. 'I'm already late for prayer, and if I don't get back they'll kill me!'

I took hold of her arms and pulled her upright. The colour drained from her face as she leaned against the bridge.

'Seriously? Get back where? Who will kill you?'

'OK, not literally.' She closed her eyes briefly and tested her weight on the foot. 'But I am petrified, because they will punish me for sure if I'm not in chapel on the dot. They'll know I've been outside without permission. Well, that's because they *never* give permission! So, let's go. *Andiamo*!'

I still had hold of her arm as she started to hobble over the bridge. This close to her I could make out several old piercings for studs in both ear lobes and a couple of fine strands of blonde hair trying to escape the white cap under her veil.

'You're English?' I asked. 'I thought I heard you speaking Italian just now?'

'Half English. Born here, brought up in London. Came back here to try to see my family and take up my vocation.' An even stronger flush rose from her throat right over her cheekbones as she stopped dead. 'You heard me talking? You were spying on me just now in the *campo*? Oh God! She sent you! I'm done for!'

'Don't be so silly! A spy? *Moi*?' I dropped my hands in exasperation. 'Being a spy would be much more fun than the dull reality, I promise you. I'm just a tourist. I've never seen you in my life before. So how could I spy on you?'

She shrugged, still eyeing me suspiciously. Her shoulders were so slight.

'Mother Superior, Mother Marta – she's capable of anything.'

'In fact if you must know I'm on business buying glass for my shop in London. So it's all perfectly *bona fide*. Nothing cloak-and-dagger about me.'

Her pout turned into a weak smile. We paused a little longer for her to get her breath, then picked up speed descending the bridge. She turned right along another narrow pavement, then through another archway similar to the one where I'd seen my stalker. By now I was even more lost than before.

'But in answer to your accusation, yes.' I couldn't resist it. 'I saw you there, scuttling out of that house, swearing at someone called Carlos, was it? The guy in the window?'

'Carlo.'

'The guy you were shagging just now like there's no tomorrow?'

'Shagging?' There was a catch in her voice. She bent her head and tried to quicken her pace. 'I don't know what you mean!'

'Oh, you understand me perfectly, Sister. I'm just putting two and two together. You are forbidden to leave the convent, but you absconded to be with your lover. He was fucking your brains out and you were loving it! I heard everything. The groaning, the bed creaking and banging against the wall, his voice, your voice – I have to admit it was a bit of a turn-on, all that *je t'aime* stuff in the middle of a dull afternoon when you haven't had some for a while. Really X-rated! I'm amazed you didn't have the whole city listening in! You have well and truly jumped the wall, haven't you?'

'Stop it! Stop it! You're mistaken!' She stopped abruptly again and pulled me round to face her. No longer the cute dolly. Her blue eyes sparked with a strange wild fire. 'And keep your voice down, please, *signora*. So, thank you for helping me, but I have to go now!'

'Hang on! I came over because I need you to help *me*!'

'I don't have time. I can't help you. Can't even help

myself.' She shrugged me off and started to walk away, but soon she stumbled, whimpering with pain. When I caught up with her she slumped against me, helpless again. 'Please! If you come back with me you can't tell them where I was or what I was doing or they'll thrash me to kingdom come!'

I bit my lip in disbelief.

'I'll keep my mouth shut on one condition. That you spill it all out to me.'

She shook her head, tucking imaginary strands of hair behind her ears and tugging the hood over her veil. A blast of cold air whistled round the corner, and we shrank back into a doorway.

I tried again. 'Sister, tell me what's wrong. Something is bothering you, I can tell, and I'm extremely good at keeping secrets.' I lowered my voice. 'You can use me as your confessor, if you like.'

A tear sparkled in the corner of her eye. I swear if I didn't know better I'd have had her down as some kind of actress. Because it got me right where it was supposed to. I was already putty in her hands.

'They're tugging me every which way. Him, and them. They're all ripping me in half!'

Now I couldn't help smiling. 'Calm down with the melodramatics, honey. It can't be that bad.'

She hesitated, then clasped her hands together. 'Carlo, he's my old boyfriend, you see, from when I was young.

We bumped into each other last summer, just before I was going in to the convent, literally when I was on my way there. I had just left my family. Well, my cousins. The others won't speak to me. I was saying goodbye.'

'Goodbye?'

I decided to be patient, almost unheard of for me. After all, it hadn't taken much persuasion for her to pour her heart out. It would be worth it just to hear what else had been going on up there in that bedroom.

She was quiet for a moment so we restarted our snail's pace, past tourists studying maps, workers carrying briefcases, a crocodile of children coming home from school. On a wider stretch of canal a barge chugged past us, a grand piano lashed to its deck. Nobody looked at us. Two women, deep in conversation, a nun and a sharp-looking businesswoman – what was to notice?

'It's a closed order. We are not allowed to speak to outsiders except through a grille. It's silent, and it's bliss. We're not even allowed to speak to our Sisters unless we're working, and then we chatter like starlings though we're not supposed to. We're not even supposed to have favourite friends, though of course we do. I work in the winery. I have just produced my own label. *La Religieuse*. I trained as a wine taster in London, you see. It's very potent, and pre-order sales have already meant they can afford to restore the frescoes in the chapel.'

'Yes, yes, enough already about all that. What I want

to know is, if it's all such bliss in there why do you keep running away to see Carlo?'

That flush as she considered the question. Those parted lips. Having heard what sounds she could make I could easily imagine that lovely face melting as she flung herself in ecstasy under the muscular body of her lucky boyfriend. It must be like Christmas every day for him when he heard the secret knock, saw his hooded visitor at the door, when he pulled her into his grotty little house and unpeeled her cumbersome clothes to get to the white nakedness beneath. Her pale thighs opening for him on that creaking bed, him falling on top of her, pushing himself inside her, the shadows falling upon their writhing, bucking bodies ...

I sat her down gently on the steps of a church. Hell, I was the one who needed to sit down. We watched some old men in a workshop hammering and moulding various slim pieces of wood to form the curved ribs of a gondola.

'I told you! I'm torn between the two! I love him, but I love my Sisters and my other life, too. It's what I have chosen. One day soon I'll either be locked in for good. Or locked right out.'

'So how did this thing with Carlo start over?'

She swallowed and stared back the way we'd come. 'I'd said my farewells and I was walking along the beach on the Lido, trying to calm myself down before I took the *vaporetto* back to the city, and there was Carlo coming out of the sea like some kind of god. When I last saw him he was a skinny teenager and now he's, oh God, he's all man, he was in these tight swimming shorts, really tanned and muscled, big shoulders.'

'Big everything?'

A little snuffle of laughter escaped her. She clapped her hand over her mouth. 'Yes! You couldn't miss it! And there was me trudging along, no make-up, hair already chopped off, eyes red from crying.'

'He saw you in this get-up?' I plucked at her skirt, expecting her to slap my hand away. I lifted it a little. Her ankles were dainty in the hideous shoes. I lifted the skirt a little higher. I couldn't stop myself. And she didn't stop me. Higher, and I saw that she was wearing thick black stockings, which should have been ugly but were enticing in a St Trinian's kind of way, and even more so when I saw that they were fastened at the top by black suspenders. My stomach gave a surprised clench of desire at the sight of her smooth white flesh above the industrial-strength wool. I had a mad urge to see what kind of knickers a nun would wear, but belatedly she slapped my hand away.

'Oh, this isn't a proper habit. This is just for novices, and they make it as scratchy and hot as hell. But I always wore very plain clothes, no jewellery, no heels. No adornment at all.' She sighed. I smelt sweet, chocolatey breath. 'I hadn't looked at a guy for years. Not been interested. I guess it made the call from God all the easier to answer.'

The way she said it made it believable. If I had to listen to someone banging on about a call from God while sitting in a pub in Clapham or on a rooftop bar in Manhattan I'd have snorted with derision. But sitting here on the steps of this church in a corner of this magical maze of a city? Listening to this very real, almost petulant girl? Being called by God somehow made perfect sense, however inconvenient it must have been. I felt a physical tug to get closer.

'So how old are you? You look too young to have been struggling with this, this *call*, for years.'

'I'm twenty-three. Nearly twenty-four.' She pulled herself up like a little soldier and something in my heart gave way a little more. 'And I was – I am – more than ready.'

'Go on, Sister. I want all the details of this wicked assignation.' I nudged her. 'It'll make you feel so much better.'

'He'd changed so much, but he recognised me instantly.'

'Your face is the same.'

'Oh, *signora*! That's exactly what he said!' She clasped my arm with her little fingers. 'Oh God, those old feelings came rushing back, even though he was the one who hurt me! He was my first – my last – and I was trembling, churning stomach, weak knees, breathlessness, and he was right in front of me, and he knew, he told me later, he knew exactly what I was planning to do, he

27

could tell from my horrible clothes and hair and also the grave expression on my face, and that's why he barely said a word, he just dragged me off the beach into this little hut where he'd been painting tourist portraits all summer, just a few blankets, cooking stove, glasses, beer, and we just kissed and kissed, and his mouth and his tongue pushing in and he practically had a beard, oh, I had such a scratched sore chin when I finally got to Santa Maria!'

I presumed that was the convent and the name was like a cold shower over both of us.

'Tell me, Sister,' I urged her, pressing my hand on her thigh. 'Offload all this angst. Indulge an embittered old bag and tell me!'

'You're not an old bag, *signora*! You're so beautiful!'

Now it was my turn to blush.

She absently put her hand over mine. Her breath was coming quickly. 'It had been so long, we didn't talk at all, then I was down on the floor, and my skirt was right up over my, you know, and he undid my shirt, oh, he used to love my, my breasts, the first time he touched them he was like a boy with candy, he used to suck my nipples for hours like they were sweets, we had so much time when we were younger, and I love that feeling, it makes me want him so badly, and he's changed, you see, he really is a man now, he's been working out, he's had

28

other girls, he's much tougher, much stronger, not so, what, *tentative*, quite the reverse, he was determined and in a hurry and anyway his swim shorts, well, they came off easily, and there it was, his beautiful cock standing up so stiff and ready, even bigger than I remembered, and, oh, God forgive me, I should have stopped him then, everything was telling me I should stop it, I was late, the Sisters were expecting me, like I'm late now, I had to stop it, but I was so wet and he was rock hard and then he –'

'Go on!' I was holding her hand tightly, almost pleading with her to continue. 'How did it feel when he fucked you?'

'He just thrust inside me once, that's all it took, and then we both came like an explosion. I screamed. It was almost the last sound I was allowed to make for weeks after.' She closed her eyes and tipped her face up towards the grey sky and stuck the tips of her fingers into her mouth as if to silence herself. 'It made me feel like a virgin all over again.'

She opened her eyes and we stared at each other. Her words fell round us like petals. Madonna sang a song once about being touched for the very first time, but this was sexier than anything I'd ever heard. And I knew exactly what this young woman meant. It made me want to be a virgin all over again, too.

Not really thinking, I took her fingers away from her

29

mouth and kissed them, one by one. She watched me, watched my mouth, watched her hands as I laid them down in her lap.

'You've told me all this,' I said hoarsely. 'But I still don't know your name.'

'Natalia. Sister Benedicta. When I was outside I was Natalia.' She snatched my wrist and looked at my watch. 'Enough talking. Enough questions! I must hurry. I'm going to lose him, I'm going to lose the convent. It's all going to be a disaster!'

'Let's go, then.' I cursed myself for breaking the spell. I helped her along an even narrower alley. It was dark now, and my feet were killing me, too. Lights and sounds were booming from what sounded like a big open space not far away.

'They're preparing for the Carnivale in the piazza,' she murmured, waving her free hand vaguely.

'Perhaps I can think up some excuse for why you're late. Say it was my fault in some way.'

She looked at me and her eyes were huge like a Manga cartoon.

'You'd do that? But you said you needed my help?'

I laughed. 'I only need you to tell me the way back to my hotel. I was totally lost back there, you see. And then I found you.'

Another silence surrounded us, this time like a shroud, tucking us into our private corner. Even the distant music thumped like a heartbeat. Totally lost, that was it. And I was still lost, looking into those amazing big eyes, childish and helpless, asking for my help, still backlit with that strange sexy fire that told me she was harder than she looked and knew more than I did. I wondered how long it would take before she pulled away from me. But she didn't move. She was staring, too. What did she see? An older, more knackered version of herself, perhaps, with green eyes instead of blue, more laughter lines, but blonde like her, slim like her, sex-mad like her ...

She started to speak, but bit into that luscious pink lower lip again and instead leaned against me. I let my arm steal round her waist. The warmth of the thick fabric outlined her hidden curves and it had now gone from strangely comforting to slowly arousing, holding her close to me as we made slow progress round another corner and I recognised the glass showroom I had visited earlier that day. I caught the eye of the proprietor as we hurried past it, wondering what Signora Martelli would think seeing the hard-nosed buyer from London tottering along the street arm in arm with a beautiful nun.

'Hey, another thing you haven't told me, Natalia. If everything's so rosy between you, why were you arguing with Carlo just now?'

She shook her head. Her ankle must have been feeling better, because she diverted us briskly round the back of the shops.

'Go on. We're friends now, aren't we?'

She glanced at me. Her eyelashes were so long. 'He's been getting rough with me. Rougher than usual.'

She stopped beneath an old, crumbling wall. Dry ivy spilled over it and a large looming building cast its shadow from the garden inside.

'Natalia? I can help you, remember?'

'We're here,' she muttered, pointing at a tiny wooden door in the wall. 'This is Santa Maria Convent.'

I lifted her chin.

'Tell me what he did to you.'

'Oh, *bella signora*! Don't worry, it's nothing like that.' She shook her head. 'He didn't hurt me. I liked it. But some of the things he makes me do – I know it's because he wants me to love what we do, get addicted, so much that I won't be able to stop. So much that I'll have to leave the convent.'

'So why the argument?'

'The usual. Trying to persuade me to stay with him. The stupid thing is our life together is just like being in the convent, now. We have to stay indoors. We can never go out, in case someone sees us … He went too far, that's all. Over the top. And I got angry. As you saw.'

We both jerked up our heads like a pair of reindeer at a quiet rustling sound inside the garden behind us: leaves, or footsteps – we couldn't tell. No one was passing along the alleyway.

'You can tell me anything, Sister.'

I liked the way that sounded. She paused. I could swear I heard someone clear their throat behind the door, but I kept my eyes on her.

'OK. But only because I'll never see you again. He went on so long today, made me drink wine and water all afternoon, wouldn't let me go to the toilet, and then he made me lie on my stomach so that I was pressing down on my bladder and there was this swelling, stinging sensation, actually it felt good, but then he took me from behind, all the time pressing his hands on my stomach, and he fucked me until the piss started to come, it was trickling hot down my legs, on to the bed, and I was getting embarrassed trying to stop it, but he was laughing and then I was starting to come as well, and I couldn't tell the difference because it was this hot building sensation and then as I came I totally pissed myself and it was such a relief and an amazing climax and he was shouting with pleasure, he loved it, but it was all a big messy gush but then it felt wet and dirty and when it stopped I was totally humiliated. I was furious with him!'

I gave a low whistle. 'You got me there, girl. Even *I'm* a little – OK, I'm shocked by that!'

'You see? I have to decide. I have to leave him.'

She pushed her face close to me, daring me to stop her I think. She was so close that I moved a little and our lips brushed tantalisingly. Again we paused, our lips warm and damp against each other. I wanted to go further and kiss her. I had never kissed a woman on the mouth, but it was like the Katy Perry song. I wanted to kiss a girl I'd met less than an hour ago because I knew I would like it.

But the girl said, 'And now I have to leave *you*.'

Something like panic gripped me. 'You don't have to go in there, Natalia. Come with me to my hotel. Leave them, leave him, come with me back to London!'

A smile tugged at her lips, and I felt a crazy urge to giggle. It sounded mad, but marvellous! This beautiful girl, by my side, coming home with me from Venice like a glittering, glorious souvenir. 'It's more complicated than that – oh, I don't know *your* name!'

'I'm Jennifer. And it doesn't have to be complicated. What's the point of going in there and saying your prayers when you just want to be free?'

'But I need to be in there, too!' She put her hand on the door, resting it there as if it had a heartbeat. 'I love being in here. It's tugging at me now, physically tugging me to come back. Already Carlo, the memory of his kiss, his touch, his body, it's all gone –' she flicked her fingers dismissively '– and now I'm home.'

'You're not dismissing me as well!' I took her by the arms, forcefully this time. Her head fell back and her veil slipped very slightly so that now I could see silky strands of hair falling into her eyes. 'Come with me, now, Natalia! Just do it!'

She opened that luscious mouth and I'm certain she was going to say something amazing like 'Great idea! I'm there!' but instead she squealed and suddenly stumbled awkwardly backwards through the little door, which had swung wide open. I tripped over her and fell into the garden too, still holding on to her, and then just as suddenly the door slammed shut behind us.

We were in a small dark garden with starved-looking lemon trees standing around like statues but giving off an unusually strong scent for winter. Illuminated at the far end was a marble statue of the Virgin Mary, hands together and eyes cast to heaven.

'I haven't got time for this.' I let go of her irritably. 'What is it, Natalia? Why are you making silly faces at me?'

But her eyes just went wide as if she was scared.

'They used to call these convents the pleasant prison, didn't they? Girls who didn't have the call, but were just plonked here by their fathers because they had no prospects.'

Natalia was mouthing something at me, but I reckoned she was just teasing. 'Well, you're welcome to it. If you want to stay here, that's your funeral, or wedding, or whatever. Just tell me the way back to the Danieli Hotel, and I'm outta here.'

I turned towards the gate. An enormous, rough-looking man was barring the way. I couldn't see his features in the darkness, but he was tall and broad, arms crossed and legs planted far apart, and he was holding some kind of rake or hoe. He jabbed his finger towards Natalia.

'What's his problem? Why doesn't he say something?'

'He's deaf. He's saying we have to go inside right now.'

'Not me, sugar. I've got a business meeting to get to.'

But he shoved us both violently across the dusty garden and into the looming building, through another tiny door and up some stairs and before I could say another word we were in a kind of stark waiting room which smelt of tea and wet newspapers. There was no light, nothing but a table, a fire grate where one weak finger of flame flickered, and another enormous statue of the Virgin Mary. In the silence that followed I thought I could hear the distant sound of angelic singing.

'So the sinner returns.'

A door beside the statue opened and in walked my stalker.

Chapter Three

I screamed in fright and grabbed Natalia. But she simply stroked my arm, calming me. The tall figure was motionless, one gloved hand still holding the door open. Then Natalia stepped away from me and dropped to her knees.

'Oh, Mother Superior. Please forgive me!'

I knelt to shake her and hissed, 'Natalia! What are you doing? Christ, we have to get out of here! This guy – he's been stalking me –'

But she flung herself forwards, spreading her arms out on the floor. Her cloak and skirt rode up the back of her legs and above her white thighs I saw what knickers nuns wear. What looked like puffy cotton bloomers, the kind of thing a long-legged model might wear on the catwalk with teetering platforms and a military waistcoat.

Her little white hands touched the man's shiny black shoes poking out of his long black coat.

'Natalia! Get up!'

The stalker turned in my direction and put one hand up to silence me. No need. I was already frozen to the spot. Then he started slowly undoing the buttons from the collar in a kind of creepy striptease, over the chest, down the front. And as it fell open I caught a whiff of that smoky scent, and with a sick lurch in my stomach I remembered my fantasy. It *was* incense, and it was coming off the burning candles and silver incense burners positioned all round the room.

'So, Sister Benedicta.'

Natalia raised her head from the floor. 'Yes, Mother?'

I stared, aghast, as the hat and coat came off and the stalker was not a man at all. At least, the figure was dressed as a nun, so presumably it was female. But she was still very masculine. Tall, thin, with an almost translucent white face, slightly hooked nose and large, glittering black eyes. She kept these eyes on me as she directed the inevitable question at Natalia.

'Where have you been?'

Natalia's eyes filled with tears. She said nothing.

'She's been with me!' My voice clanged in the dank room. 'I was lost in one of the back streets, and she helped me.'

The Mother Superior handed her disguise to a second

nun with freckles and a dimple whose comely figure had glided silently into the room. She folded the clothes and held them in front of her, waiting. There was a long silence punctuated only by a bell tolling somewhere in what sounded like Morse code. It was as if they had all the time in the world. The angelic singing, which was louder now, trailed through the still open door beside the statue.

'You're lying. I don't know who you are, *signora*, but you are evidently a woeful influence. I know exactly where, and with whom, Sister Benedicta has been. Not just today, but several times before.'

I clamped my lips shut. So, not stalking me at all. Stalking my little Natalia.

Mother Marta picked up a thin little switch from the table. I hadn't noticed it before. It was black leather, like a riding crop, and had a bunch of fine leather tassels dangling off the end. Nine tails?

'You have been out of the convent, which is forbidden, Sister. I think seven times. The seven deadly sins. That amounts to once a month since you arrived here and took your initial vows.'

I saw something shift behind Natalia's eyes as she maintained her awkward prone position on the floor. She had visited Carlo much more than once a month, I was sure of it. Clever girl.

'And you have been going into a house belonging to

Carlo Martelli, and you have been alone with him there, naked with him there, and fornicating with him there.'

Natalia's face was draining of all colour. I took a worried step towards her but the whip came down smartly in the air between us.

'You have broken every vow, committed every sin it is possible to commit whilst a member of this house. Lying to us, hiding from us, scuttling through the city like a dung beetle, speaking to others and fornicating with a man. Do you wish to stay here, or do you wish to be expelled? Either way you will be punished. You know the rules. You vowed to keep to them when you entered.'

Expelled. I wish to be expelled! I was willing Natalia to say it. This horrible woman made normal activities, normal pleasures, sound so evil and dirty. Natalia was best out of it. I was even prepared to take whatever the punishment was alongside her if she would only come away with me.

'I know the rules, Mother, and I vow to keep them. I want to stay here, Mother. And I wish to be punished in front of my Sisters.'

'No! Natalia, no!'

The whip flicked down in the air again, so close to me that my hair lifted from my forehead in its breeze. I couldn't believe it. Natalia was speaking in a low, warm voice, not a high, frightened one. She *meant* what she was saying!

'What a mere novice like you wishes is of no consequence but yes, you will go now into the chapel and prostrate yourself. And your friend's punishment can be to watch.'

Natalia nodded and stood up. She was still very white. She avoided my eye, as if I was the one who had done wrong, and walked calmly through the door. The freckled nun took my arm and led me into a long thin chapel. My eyes started streaming with the heavy scent of incense pouring out of a large silver basket swinging back and forth on a silver chain. There was a Gothic vaulted ceiling, plaster walls painted with faint, peeling frescoes, and a meshed grille running down the whole of one side. On the other side were pews, and in these pews were several more nuns and, I noticed with surprise, a priest standing behind the altar at the far end. They must have been waiting for hours. In their utter stillness they all looked like figurines.

'Prostrate yourself, Sister.'

Natalia lay down in front of the altar and spread her arms and legs in a star shape. My heart started pounding with fear. The singing was still radiating from behind the grille, but it was no longer angelic. It had descended to a low, grim humming sound. Sweat started trickling down my back, gathering in my armpits, prickling in my hair.

The freckled nun planted her feet on either side of Natalia and folded her cape and skirt right up over her

41

bottom so that I could see those awful bloomers again. Then freckle-face wrenched those down in one swift movement, right down to Natalia's knees, so that there was nothing covering her but the black stockings.

I glanced round. 'Someone stop this! It's torture!' I said, but it came out as a kind of dry squeak. The humming got louder, and no one was listening to me. They had all turned to look at Natalia, lying on the floor, her round white bottom and lovely thighs glowing in the dead, dim light of the chapel.

Mother Marta stepped forward, raised her arm, and with a swish like a wasp's wing brought the whip down on Natalia's buttocks. The sound was extraordinary. The sharp stroke on Natalia's soft flesh rang out like a cruel gunshot. The tender flesh rippled under the blow. I gasped in horror, and lunged forward, but someone else pinned my arms behind me to stop me moving. Natalia jerked involuntarily off the floor, showing a quick flash of her unwaxed pussy between her open thighs, and I saw her fingers clawing at the polished wooden floor. But she made no sound.

'Don't you move, Sister, or you get double.'

But even as she spoke so harshly, Mother Marta leaned down and stroked Natalia's butt cheek, where a livid red stripe had come up. And yet Natalia lay there as if she was asleep. A new respect for her bubbled up inside me, alongside the revulsion and hatred for the nun meting out such a caning to my powerless girl. We all watched as the nun stroked the other cheek, almost as if she was preparing it like prime steak. Then she quickly stepped back and swiped the whip down a second time, squarely on the second cheek.

Natalia turned her head slightly as her little rump jerked up again involuntarily. Again the plump flesh quivered under the blow, and again there was a tantalising glimpse of her bush as she bounced off the floor.

A kind of low sighing gasp echoed round the stone chapel. The watching nuns and priest were very still in their places, but bright-eyed, almost crazed as they gloated over the awful spectacle before them. Some nodded, and I realised that of course they recognised what was going on because it had happened to them. Who knew how often?

As a third stroke came down and the thwack resounded round the chapel, I could swear that this time Natalia's bottom stayed up even longer, as if inviting the stroke instead of recoiling from it. She moved it slightly from side to side, almost kneeling up to lift her bottom higher into the air. As I glimpsed the plump lips of her pussy tucked between her legs, the quick slash of pink cunt as she wiggled her bottom, a spike of desire shocked me, flashing through my own cunt and crouching there, so that it started to throb with wanting.

Mother Superior smacked her hard again but she had

obviously seen what I had seen because this time she shoved one foot between Sister Benedicta's already open legs before doing so, exposing that bare pussy to us all, showing us how Natalia seemed to be wriggling with pleasure.

'Now before you go into an extended forced silence, Sister, you must make your confession. Repeat your sins, in detail, and ask for penance.'

'I have broken the rules of the convent and disobeyed you, Mother.' Natalia's voice was strong and sweet in the polished silence. I was feeling dizzy from the incense, which had filled the chapel with a kind of heady fog.

'How exactly?'

Mother Superior kicked at the back of Natalia's knees, so that she went up higher on them, thrusting her bottom, decorated now with three pink stripes, into the air.

'I have followed my carnal desires, Mother, and ran away in secret to meet a man and to fornicate with him.'

Mother Superior placed the whip at the base of Natalia's bum crack, and for a moment I thought she was going to fuck her with it. She hesitated. We all waited, staring at the pink bottom, the pussy lips parting as Natalia kept it in the air, the tight little arsehole just visible in the shadowy fold. Oh God, not up the arse, I thought, my stomach twisting painfully at the realisation that I was equally appalled and excited by the thought, the incense, the humming, the swishing whip and that girl's bottom, the inviting pussy, I could almost feel the sly insertion of the whip into my own cunt. Christ, anything was possible.

Distracted, I looked at Mother Superior now, and saw that as she stroked the whip up Natalia's bum crack, almost tenderly, her chiselled face had very slightly softened, too. The high cheekbones and hooked nose made her look less like a scary stalker and now more like some stern governess or professor. I was reminded of a ballet teacher I had at school, who carried herself in just the same way: elegant, cold but utterly composed.

The whip ran down again. Up, and down the crack. I looked back at Natalia, and saw that flush in her throat, crawling up her cheeks, and the way she swallowed. She was swaying her bottom like an animal scratching in its stall, pushing it towards the whip as if she wanted it inside her.

'Go on,' barked Mother Superior.

Natalia swallowed. Her lips were wet as she started to speak again. 'I have gone to my lover's house and gone into his bedroom, and let him undress me, Mother, and I've touched his male part, his penis, Mother, to arouse him, and he's laid me down on his bed, sometimes on the floor, in the summer on the roof, and I've seen him totally naked, his beautiful manly body in all its glory –'

'Not glory, Sister. The sinful nakedness of Adam!'

The whip was in the air, swiping down on to the round butt cheek in less than a second. Four pink stripes on her bottom and now an audible groan escaped from Natalia, unashamedly orgasmic as she tipped her head, arching her back, lifting her bottom for more. And there were several answering groans from the nuns in the audience – sorry, congregation.

'Yes, Mother, and I am Eve, and I was sinful too and I gave in to temptation because it was too strong, too strong, I wanted it, I wanted to keep going back to him, I wanted the sex, Mother –' Natalia's voice rose to a scream as she almost danced on her knees there in front of us all. 'I wanted him to fuck me!'

There was a stunned silence. Even the humming behind the grille stopped. I glanced over to where the priest had stood. After all, he was the only representative of Adam in this room, wasn't he? The only one with a penis. But either he was invisible through the increasing, billowing clouds of incense or he had departed.

'And what will you do to make amends?'

Natalia bowed her head slightly, but the movement pushed her puffy little pussy out from between her legs even more. 'I will worship you once more, Mother. I will show you how much I love you, and my Sisters, and my house of holiness here. I'll be silent for as long as you tell me, and I'll demean myself on my knees.'

She waited. No one spoke.

'I'll lick the chapel clean with my tongue, Mother. I'll even lick you, Mother. I'll suck you, stroke you – just the way you like it –'

There was a rush of gasping round the chapel. I wasn't sure I'd heard right. The poor girl must be crazed with all that punishment, all the emotion, all the shame. Also I was really dizzy now. The air was heavily fragrant as if I was inhaling pure marijuana. I swayed backwards against whoever it was who had me pinned back against them, felt the surprising squash of breasts against my shoulder blades.

'You! Your name.'

Mother Superior had swivelled round to face me. I hadn't realised how close she was. Her face had resumed some of its earlier stoniness, but still there was a spot of bright red in each cheek and she was visibly breathless.

'Er, Coombs. Jennifer.'

'For the foul words Sister Benedicta has just uttered you will deliver the final punishment.'

'No way. Whip her? I can't. I won't.'

Natalia twisted round. Her eyes blazed at me. I could read her face like the proverbial book. Not only that, but I could read her mind. She wasn't scared, or cowed, or humiliated. She was euphoric! She was loving those red, sore stripes across her bottom. The jerking of her little pussy up and down on the hard wooden floor showed how excited she was by the whipping, the pain, the release.

And I fell for her even more. My own euphoria was released then, rushed through me, heating my body, making me drunk with the perverted pleasure I'd got from seeing my little nun being punished. The whip was put into my hands.

There was a ripple of tension through the chapel. All faces were turned to me through the misty incense, but instead of gravity or disgust, every face was etched, alight, with excitement. Cheeks were flushed, hands restlessly roving over habits or gripping pews. Some of the nuns had edged very close together. They weren't even bothering to hide their hands moving over each other's bodies. I could see the hems of their skirts rising as they fumbled underneath, trying to get into each other's bloomers and reach the naked, heated, forbidden skin beneath.

'Punish her, Jennifer Coombs!'

I lifted the whip and with an agonised wail I brought it down on to the red raw butt cheeks offered up to me. As the hard leather made contact with the soft, jiggling flesh, an electric shock sizzled right up my arm. The harsh stinging sound on her skin caused a violent reverberation through my body, and this time Natalia made no effort to hide her loud and obvious moans of pleasure as another red weal puckered up to join the other neat lines on her bottom. I was alight with excitement, because I felt those moans were just for me.

'Again!' cried Mother Marta, her voice cracking with excitement. 'Punish her again, Jennifer Coombs!'

So again I smacked the whip down on the wobbling butt cheeks, and again Natalia moaned, even louder, and swayed from side to side, spreading her legs wider, pushing her puffy pussy lips out towards her audience as her whole bottom glowed fiery red. Each time I whacked the whip down the buzzing up my arm burned stronger than before and seared right through my ribs to my cunt, where the spiking jabs of desire had turned to a deep throbbing and, as Mother Marta held up one finger to indicate a final blow, my insides started to melt. Yet I was hopping up and down on my aching feet, desperate to do it again and again.

'One more! This is supposed to be punishment, remember!'

There was a faint titter from somewhere in the room. Even Mother Marta was smiling as she spoke, a grim remote smile that lifted her stony face into the realms of a kind of mysterious beauty. I was totally high now on the druggy incense and the aroused audience, and my little Natalia moaning and writhing in front of me on the floor. One hand had come up brazenly between her legs and she was touching herself frantically as she waited for me to strike her, her fingers sweeping up and down her pink crack, her face tilted heavenwards as she swayed, then one finger went right up inside her. As she pushed it in and out I felt my own cunt coiling and tightening in readiness to come.

I bent over and started to stroke Natalia's bottom as Mother Superior had done, feeling where the blows had raised the hot beaten flesh into rigid weals, trying to soothe and calm it before one last blow, but as I did so Natalia grabbed my hand and rubbed it in between her legs, deep into her warm wet pussy, kept it there, spreading my fingers to feel every part of her, so wet and waiting, just like mine, all those people watching, several nuns openly kissing each other now, their tongues glistening in the dim smoky light before pushing into each other's mouths, their hands roving over the hidden curves under the unforgiving fabric of their habits, groping under their skirts, stroking and reaching between each other's thighs to get at each other.

My finger was sucked inside Natalia. I felt her cunt tighten round it, drawing it in higher and deeper, and I pushed it in further, my other fingers cupping her pussy, feeling the furls of skin, the nub of her clit, and that's when she jerked and screamed out loud, bucking back and forth on my finger as I fucked her with it, and now what was I to do with my own frustration? I had stopped caring or noticing what or who was around me. I scrabbled round on the floor, pulled her round to face me and as our lips moved like magnets to lock on to each other I took her hand and pushed it into my coat, up my skirt, hooked one finger into my soaking knickers and, oh God, she pushed her finger into me at the same time as I finger-fucked her, our mouths sucking and kissing, her little moans sweet in my ears, the cries and moans of the watching nuns intoxicating us both, and God knows what kind of sounds I was making.

My knees hurt like hell kneeling like that on the wooden floor. My feet ached after hours of traipsing the streets in my ill-advised boots, my head was swimming with that hallucinogenic incense and I was in full view of a chapel full of strange holy people, but none of it was as mind-blowing as the fact that for the first time in my world-weary life I was kissing a gorgeous girl, and she was a nun, and we were finger-fucking each other brutally, hard, I was feeling her warm tight cunt sucking at me, my cunt doing the same to her little wiggling fingers, she had done this before, surely, the way she was circling my clit with one finger, tickling other parts of me, all the while pushing, withdrawing, pushing her finger inside me and then she was shaking and so was I, keeping up with her, kissing her more forcefully, loving the taste of her tongue and lips, and then I found myself bucking against her as I came, my knees like jelly, shaking and crying as I came all over her fingers.

The moaning and sighing around us, which had

reached its own crescendo, gradually faded away, leaving only the metallic chink-chink of the silver chain as the incense burner rocked across the chapel like a pendulum.

I subsided on my haunches and we looked at each other. Natalia's face reflected my own shock at what had happened. She wasn't smiling. She wasn't speaking. It was like a mask had come down over her features. I wanted to be alone with her, talk to her about what had happened. I opened my mouth to speak but two things happened at once. The effect of the incense came down on me like a horse blanket. What did they have in that stuff? My head started pounding, and I couldn't see straight. Natalia, who seemed unaffected by the hazy atmosphere, was standing up and moving away from me.

I flailed about, trying to grab on to her, stop her, but she seemed to float like a mirage, along the aisle, into the crowd of nuns who surrounded and absorbed her until I couldn't make out one black and white habit from the next and now the chapel and everyone in it was swirling round me like a mad carousel.

So the second thing that happened was that someone yanked me to my feet.

'Time for you to go, Miss Coombs.'

Mother Superior stood in front of me. Her bony white face seemed to hover like the Cheshire Cat's, bobbing in the air like a balloon, disappearing, then reappearing slightly to one side. I was either going to faint or throw up.

'But Natalia – I want her to come with me.'

'I don't think so, *signora*. She has made her choice, and it's the right one. If anything, your disgusting display just then has only served to convince her. You are to leave here immediately and never return. You should never have been with Sister Benedicta, or even entered our hallowed house. So I trust you will never speak of this to anyone outside. Sister Antonia, please escort her out.'

The freckled nun pushed me through the dank parlour and slammed the door behind me. The cold air rushed at me and I took great lungfuls of it to try to clear my head, breathing in the sharp scent of lemon and the constant brackish smell of the nearby canals.

I was still struggling to find my way back to the hotel when I realised why I had goose bumps on my neck. I'd left behind my red scarf.

Chapter Four

The next morning I was sitting in Florian, the over-priced, over-crowded cafe in Piazza San Marco, typing up some calculations from my early-morning meeting with Signora Martelli. From my calm exterior as I concentrated in the plush, lamp-lit corner, you would have had no idea what had happened to me yesterday. In fact, I wasn't entirely sure it *had* happened. I hadn't even mentioned any of it to Hazel in our brief chat just now. She would only have snorted and told me I was finally losing my marbles.

So I told her nothing about Mother Marta, the looming convent, the dark chapel, the humming nuns, the harsh penalties and the whispered confessions, the vicious little whip, Natalia's plump bottom bouncing and pushing up begging for more, the vivid stripes of pain across her skin.

All I had to reassure me that I hadn't gone stark staring mad was the strong lingering smell of incense clinging to my hair, my clothes, my skin.

That, and the rhythmic throbbing in my sore cunt where Natalia's little fingers had so forcefully, Christ, *expertly*, found their way in to me, penetrated me, fucked me, right in front of Mother Superior and the entire gasping, moaning audience.

And it was that secret delicious throbbing that prompted me, during my meeting, casually to suss out if Signora Martelli was anything to do with Carlo. I didn't tell her how I knew of him. I simply asked her, as I sensed a new stickiness between my thighs despite the endless rigorous showers and douches I'd taken this morning, smelt my own lingering excitement, and tried not to wriggle too obviously on her uncomfortable chair, if she was related to an artist I'd heard of called Carlo.

'*Si! Si!*' Signora Martelli crossed her surprisingly shapely legs and swung one high-heeled court shoe. Her large-featured, hard face visibly softened beneath the helmet of dyed magenta hair, and she fluttered her fat beringed fingers in the air. 'Carlo Martelli is indeed my son!'

I thought of the strong, hairy hands leaning on the flower box outside his window as Carlo had sworn so brutishly at Natalia yesterday. The red scar running round one wrist. The loud abandoned cries they had made when fucking each other's brains out in his house, how they grunted like animals, how he sounded like an athlete, how Natalia confessed to Mother Marta and all her Sisters that they'd done it on the floor, on the roof, how rough he'd been with her, yesterday making her piss all over herself. What would mama say?

Wriggling uncontrollably now, I looked at the over-weight body encased in turquoise silk sitting like a queen in her throne, and the over-made-up face of Signora Martelli. I really was desperate now, dwelling on other people's sex lives. I could hear Hazel saying that I was a liability, what I needed was a damn good rogering, by anyone, anyhow, anywhere, and I needed it right now.

So I tried to distance myself from thoughts of Carlo and Natalia but made it even worse by focusing bizarrely on Signora Martelli and the sex she must have had to conceive her precious son. I could see a cavernous room, lit badly and unflatteringly with too-bright overhead bulbs in tatty fringed shades, lots of mahogany furniture and holy pictures and ancestral portraits all over the walls, heavy curtains, a veined marble floor, shutters banging open and closed against the Venetian night, and a huge four-poster bed draped in some kind of medieval tapestry where all the Martellis were born, copulated, and died.

I hid my smirk by swallowing the last cold drops of cappuccino she had made me. I reckoned the Signora would be the dominant one. She and Signor Martelli would be like a seaside postcard, her huge breasts bouncing heavily then squashing the deliriously happy face of Carlo's father between them, forcing one big nipple into his mouth while she clambered on top of him and straddled him with a gutteral groan, her big buttocks wobbling and squeezing over his feebly kicking legs as her wet vagina gobbled up his stiff little dick, her hair its natural black colour back then, flying down her wide back as she arched and whooped like a cowboy and the ancient wooden bed squeaked and groaned across the marble floor as she yelled at him to get bigger, go harder, go faster, ordered him to spurt it all inside her.

Now I felt slightly sick.

'And he is a very talented artist, both in oil and in glass.' Signora Martelli bulldozed my thoughts and tapped a huge frame on her desk with one long red fingernail. It showed a stony-faced young man in a university gown and mortar board, looking like every other surly graduate who wishes his parents would stop taking bloody photos and bugger off so he can go party with his mates. 'He used to work for the company until he started to get commissions for his frescoes but then he gave it all up – but enough about him. Why don't you come to Murano this afternoon and we can itemise your order?'

As we made arrangements for me to go over to the

island, I felt relief at the normality of talking business and also that, if Carlo Martelli did exist, large as life and twice as hairy, then so did everyone else from last night's scenario. All those strange sights and sounds and voices and commands and punishments and Natalia's fingers, oh, her sweet little fingers, were, after all, totally real. They weren't the figment of some feverish dream.

And yet, and yet. I was still distracted when I left the meeting in Signora Martelli's glittering little shop near San Marco. I should have been glad to get back to normal, get on with what I did best, doing business and making money. So why could I not shake off this disorientation? Hadn't I had a lucky escape from that holy hellhole? Why, when I had eventually found my way back to the Danieli last night and stumbled up to my swagger bedroom, safe from the clouds of mind-bending incense, the gloomy chanting of sins and the vicious thwack of the cat o'nine tails – *why* did I feel as if I'd been cast out?

I shut my iPad and opened my guidebook listlessly to read about historical visitors to Venice. Casanova, who was having sex with two sisters, both nuns ... Lord Byron, whose lover threw herself into the Grand Canal when he dumped her. Georges Sand, who stayed in the Danieli and went off with the doctor who tended her sick lover. What made me smile eventually was the hilarious statistic that in the mid-seventeenth century there

were as many nuns in Venice as there were prostitutes
… What on earth kind of city was this?

I glanced around the famous *caffe*. In the winter the
clientele in here were mostly understated, elegant Italians,
women with perfectly pinned chignons and silk scarves
artfully tied round their necks, men with cashmere
sweaters over their shoulders in a way no Englishman
could ever carry off. I tried to imagine the place seething
with the gaudy courtesans of old in their tight bodices,
huge skirts, breasts bulging as they lounged on the knees
of groping men in wigs and breeches, all the debauchery
these gilded walls had seen. Everything was mirrored,
with lights burning like torches in gold lamps, and in
the air the aroma of hot chocolate was mixed with sweet
Marsala.

The windows were steamed up. I rubbed at the glass
to stare out at the misty piazza. People were stepping in
single file across the duckboards set up above the *acqua
alta* that once again had swirled in from the lagoon.

I looked at my watch. I had better visit another supplier
or two before I went over to Murano.

A flurry of femininity erupted in the corner of my eye.
A group of about six nuns in long black habits, their
faces framed and minimised by squares of white starch,
whisked through a painted panel in the wall beside me,
whispering and tittering behind their hands. Surely any
kind of communication was forbidden, certainly any kind

of hilarity? But no one else glanced up. Groups of twittering nuns must be quite common around here.

But what surely wasn't so common was how *young* these all were! My heart clattered in my chest as I instinctively scanned the group for Natalia, even though I was fairly sure these sisters were dressed differently. I hadn't really been able to see the other nuns in the smoky dark chapel last night, let alone gauge their ages, but I had supposed them to be around my age or older. These girls were fresh-faced and slim, barely out of school. Younger even than Natalia. Anyway, she wasn't amongst them. I shrank back in my seat, embarrassed by my blatant eagerness.

Get over it, Jennifer. You've got work to do.

Even so, there was a chance one of them might recognise me. But their wide wimples blocked out the world. They only had shining, excited eyes for each other, and in seconds the door had closed softly behind them.

I drained my glass of entrails-simmering sambuca and without thinking dashed outside before the nuns were swallowed up in the throng of the chilly square. To my right was the baroque swell of San Marco, its golden facade, buttresses, domes and arches all swooping and soaring like an amazing wedding cake. To my left was the colonnaded end of the square, leading to more shops and hotels, and that's where I saw those black and white figures again. They were like little chess pieces. And they looked as if they were playing hopscotch like a bunch of schoolgirls. But closer up I realised they were dancing from foot to foot because they had no stockings or shoes on. Either a punishment, or a requirement, or just sensible when the rest of us were getting wet feet in the high tide.

At some kind of signal they all turned and filed out of the square, heads bowed, holding their skirts tantalisingly high over slim white – and bare – legs as they splashed delicately through the greenish-grey waters of the Adriatic. As I followed behind, keeping to the edge of the streets where it was slightly dryer, I thought I must still be hallucinating: not only did these girls seem virtually to be walking on water, but they all had gold tattoos, in a motif I couldn't make out at this distance, winding up one delicate ankle.

I doggedly followed until I realised we had reached the narrow alleyway with the crumbling wall, the dry trailing ivy and the little door, and was so engrossed in my thoughts that I jumped when one of the nuns stopped and put her hand on my arm.

'You look lost.' I could feel the heat of her skin through my suede coat. 'And you look exhausted, Sister.' She had glittering black eyes, a warm, round face, and a strong Italian accent.

At the word 'Sister' I almost collapsed and let her pull me closer to her. The others glided up and gazed at me. Was it the starch of their veils making them incline their heads stiffly, like ducks, or was it some kind of holy deportment drummed into them?

'Do you have somewhere to go?' another one asked.

'You're not supposed to talk, are you?' I asked faintly. 'You're supposed to be silent.'

There was that ripple of amusement again.

'We're from Santa Monica Convent. We have different clothing, you see? Black habits, not grey, with these big wimples. The Sisters in here are silent. We are allowed to speak, but we are not really allowed to see. We do the sewing for Santa Maria and we bring them supplies. Also this morning we are visiting for a retreat with Father Luca.'

They closed ranks, pushing me as part of their shoal along the narrow street and up to the door. I froze. What did I think I was doing here? And what kind of reception was I going to get if I went inside?

'You didn't say what the problem was,' the nun said softly as I tried to back away.

'Problem?'

They all gathered round me, those pretty heads tilted patiently. I looked up at the looming building behind the wall, the big cross glinting on the roof, the ivy, the little door. Heard that angelic singing again.

'I want to go inside. I *need* to. There's someone, a Sister, I want to see. But they won't let outsiders in, and they certainly won't allow me anywhere near. They think I will lead her astray.'

'Well, you are a woman of the world, we can all see that. You are a terrible danger to them.'

'I just want to see her. OK, just speak to her. Sister Benedicta. I want to help her.' I blinked back surprising tears. 'Please, Sisters. Can you smuggle me in with you?'

They gazed at me beadily, like a flock of blackbirds, then all nodded in unison. One of them took a folded habit and veil out of a bag. Of course. They'd been sewing. Another one pulled my jacket off. I stood still, helpless, while little hands whisked efficiently under my skirt to unhook my stockings and roll them quickly down, dragged off my boots.

'You must have bare feet.'

And all at once I was one of them, trussed up in my own big, stiff wimple and the heavy black dress bulky over my own clothes. My jacket and shoes were in a bag hidden under a pile of honey-smelling candles. The gardener opened the gate and we glided into the building. I couldn't see a thing, blinkered as I was on either side and keeping my eyes down, but I still stalled, heart beating with fear, when we reached the dank-smelling parlour.

'Sister Perpetua here wishes to make confession before retreat. We know Father Luca is busy, and also Mother Superior. Is it possible she can make it to someone else, perhaps through the special Sisters in Sin grille? I know it's for those who have transgressed most horribly and most recently. Perhaps Sister Benedicta has come out of solitary?'

I had no idea who my saviour was speaking to, or how she knew Natalia was being punished, but I kept my head right down as we padded on our bare feet over the polished floor of the chapel. All I could hear was the faint singing somewhere behind me, then warm hands pushed me down on to my knees in front of an arched grille, and suddenly I was alone.

There was a rustle of skirts on the other side of the grille and an impatient sigh.

'Sister Perpetua? I am Sister Benedicta. I will hear your confession, but you know I cannot speak further.'

My head swam. All I'd had was sambuca and coffee and Signora Martelli's silly little hard *biscotti* for breakfast, and now all the incense was making me feel peculiar.

'Is that you, Natalia?' I croaked.

There was a gasp. I strained to see through the grille. I could make out a shape, the oval pepperpot shape of her head and veil, but that was all. I put my hands on the cold iron mesh.

'Natalia, it's me. Jennifer. The Santa Monica sisters smuggled me in. I want to see you. After yesterday – are you all right? Have I got you into trouble? Are you in pain after that beating? I feel so lost out here. I want to touch you so much, Natalia.' I swallowed. 'Tell me if you don't want this, and I'll go away.'

'Stop, Jennifer. This is all wrong. So wrong.' It was a whisper, but I could feel it shivering on my cheek. She was right up close on the other side. 'I feel the same, but it's wicked. I'm no good.'

'Nor am I. That's why we need to be together. Away from –'

It all became so clear to me as I uttered the words. I needed to get her away, not just from Carlo and his mother, Natalia's unforgiving family, my work, my empty love life, Hazel, but away from the whole world.

'You want to come in here, with me? With only the Sisters, in silence, for ever?'

Her breath was warm. I blew through the grille, and she blew back. I could drink it. Literally. Today it smelt strongly of a very sweet, very intoxicating wine.

'For ever, for now, who knows? Just that, darling, I want to get in there with you. After yesterday, the way it felt when you, you, touched me, remember? In the chapel?'

There was a pause. 'When I put my fingers in you?'

Oh God. My knees trembled as I tried to stay upright.

'I want to do it to you, but in private, just us, I want to do the same thing, and much much more, so that you know how it feels, very gently, I want to kiss you and I want to put my fingers inside you and feel how warm and soft and wet you are in there.'

Again, that head-swimming thing, my voice saying things I didn't know it wanted to say.

'Oh God, Jennifer! You're so lovely, so wicked! Turning me on just saying those things!'

'So let me in and I'll show you, darling. I'll kiss you first, then I'll lick you with my tongue, and then I'll stroke you, I'll take off everything you're wearing little by little and I'll kiss you on your neck, on your gorgeous breasts, I want to see them and then I want to kiss them, then everything will lead to that special place between your lovely legs.'

'I knew it.' She gave a long, shivering sigh. 'You are too dangerous, Jennifer. This is sinful. I will go to hell for this.'

'So let me in, somehow, and if you don't want me to do it I'll go. Immediately. And you'll never see me again. I just want to know if you're all right before I go back to London.'

There was a long pause. My heart thumped dully in my chest. There was another rustle of skirts. She was standing up. She was leaving. She would shut me out of her life any minute now. And then to my amazement there was a rush of dusty air and the wall between us opened. Just like that. Like a door. And there she was, my little Natalia, her heart-shaped face, blue eyes blazing, lips wet with excitement, all the more innocent and beautiful framed with the grey veil.

She pulled me through into a kind of tiny dark cell then along a pitch-black corridor and into another tiny cell, and locked the door behind us.

She looked at me. At the huge wimple like one of those cones you put on dogs to stop them biting. The black habit. My bare feet. She bit her lip and smiled.

'Sister Perpetua,' she whispered. 'You are a very naughty nun!'

We put our hands over our mouths and giggled. Then Natalia staggered slightly, and fell back on to the narrow iron bed.

'Are you ill, sweetie?'

Natalia's long eyelashes fluttered and she half opened her eyes. The corner of her mouth lifted. 'Been fasting, Jennifer. To purge myself.'

'Don't be so silly. They've been brainwashing you!'

I pulled the borrowed habit and veil off me, and threw them both to the floor.

'Impure thoughts about you, Jennifer,' said Natalia softly. 'Wicked. Evil. And all that flagellation has done me no good at all, because here come those thoughts all over again.'

I held my breath. Natalia's eyes were wide open now, blue as sapphires, and full of tears. My body went hot as I stared down at her. Something about the look of innocence hiding all that sin, something about the helpless way she lay there, something about the way it made me feel so strong. I smoothed my hand over her face. My body was weak as water. Natalia didn't move, but we were both panting, mouths open. The tip of Natalia's

67

little pink tongue was resting on her teeth, bubbles of saliva on her pale lips. Feathery wisps of hair stuck out of the white cap.

I couldn't stand it. I plucked at the veil and wrenched it off her.

'I want to see your hair, Sister!'

Natalia flinched as if she'd been stung, scrabbling to cover her head, and I saw why. Apart from one or two strands the golden hair had been hacked crudely into a crew cut, even shorter than yesterday. Another punishment. I lifted Natalia's hands away from her face.

'It's still beautiful. *You're* still beautiful.'

But I was feeling less gentle now. Maybe it was the brutal haircut making her look harder. I pushed the young nun back on to the hard bed, trapping her hands up above her head. Natalia resisted and wriggled underneath me, her blue eyes flashing, and in the strange hushed atmosphere we found ourselves in, so cold, so dark, so silent, so far away from everything as if we had rushed down a long dark tunnel, I understood that flash. I could feel it in response, nipping at my insides. I was inside a convent now, supposedly sacred, but here was the snake-bite of temptation.

Natalia let out a long, harsh breath, as if it was her last. We stopped wrestling, and she went very still. I could sense Natalia, the nun, her warm body underneath me. But she was invisible. Not the curve of her breasts.

Not the swell of her bottom. Nothing at all under that heavy habit.

I felt tight like a violin string. Bones and skin vibrating like flies' wings. Everything inside me was loosening. But I knew I had to be careful. Whatever Natalia had done with Carlo, my guess was that she had never had sex with another woman. And I was damned if I was going to let on that I was a lesbian virgin, too! I rested my mouth on Natalia's, softly, and pressed a little, waiting for her to push me off or screech, but still she lay there quietly.

'I want you, Natalia! Even just speaking to you just then turned me on. I want you so much!'

In answer she twined her fingers in my long hair and pulled my head down, crushed my mouth, opened her lips softly, as if she was breathing me in. That lovely smell of sweet wine, and something else, mints? I rolled on to my side, so that we were face to face, arms tight around each other, my bare legs tangled with the nun's heavy skirt, kicking between her woollen stockings.

Natalia's cool white hands were already up under my shirt, stroking up my hot skin, under my bra strap, pressing my breasts, but I couldn't feel any part of her body. I fumbled with her habit but all I found was endless buttons and folds and hooks and swathes of material, and I started to tear at it.

'Stop, *cara*, stop. Don't rip it!' Natalia batted me away. 'I can't go back into prayers in tatters!'

'So don't go back in there.' I felt as if a bucket of cold water had splattered over me. I let go and rolled on to my back. I was shivering with excitement and frustration and fury. A pulse was throbbing between my legs, fire flickering through that sore place. 'Come away with me.'

'I thought you wanted to stay in here with me? Which is it to be?'

I screwed my eyes up furiously. 'I don't know anything any more.'

There was a pause. 'Open your eyes. Watch me, Jenni.'

Natalia was kneeling above me, and I saw that with her pale fingers my little nun was undoing her buttons. Tossing aside the bib that covered her front, the apron, exposing more buttons round her neck.

'Let me do these ones.' I knelt up behind and undid the endless tiny buttons down the back, and pulled her dress down, then unlaced the undershirt, and underneath that were surgical-looking linen bandages, binding and flattening my darling's chest.

Natalia turned round to face me. We were both shaking now. My knees were buckling. My pussy was weeping into my knickers. I took hold of the hideous bandages and forced myself to take it slow. The nun's mouth was open, her white teeth biting into her lip, as I unwound the cruel covering. It occurred to me that Carlo must do this, every time she visits him, and get a massive hard-on. My own breasts bulged and swelled with excitement and then I whipped away the last bandage and there they were, Natalia's breasts, firm and pale and soft, her nipples slowly changing colour from pale pink to an urgent, dark, red.

'Let me, now,' whispered Natalia, and much more easily she pulled my shirt off, quickly unhooked ny bra, and caught my bigger breasts as they fell into her hands. We knelt in front of each other on the bed, feeling each other's breasts, our breath coming in uneven gasps of longing.

Natalia's fine, delicate features blurred and fused as she came closer and her fingers stroked my bare breasts, my back, my legs under the tight pencil skirt, sending ripples of pleasure through me. Somehow the balance of power had shifted, but I didn't give a damn. I closed my eyes, letting my head droop backwards as the soft caresses lulled me. I realised how tired I was. Then Natalia's mouth bumped up against mine. We both waited, mouths just touching. My breath stopped totally. I couldn't move away. My lips softened and parted. Natalia rubbed her mouth harder against mine. I slid my hands under the nun's heavy skirt, felt the white skin on top of those ugly black stockings, the voluminous cotton bloomers still there, and felt a violent kick of desire inside me.

As Natalia's tongue flicked inside my mouth I pushed her down again, sucking her tongue in between my teeth, so that our faces moulded together and our bare breasts and hard nipples were rubbing against each other, our bodies tangling together.

This would be enough, I thought. This kissing. Perhaps if this is all, we won't have sinned. Natalia can go back inside the convent, and I'll go back to London, and no one will ever know. But it was like setting a taper to a candle as we feasted on each other. We couldn't stop this. No way.

And those violent urges kept on coming. This must be how men feel, I reckoned, when they want to fuck. I lifted Natalia's skirt up and there were the voluminous white cotton bloomers. I stroked my hand over them, over the mound of Natalia's pussy. Natalia squealed, and smacked at my hand, but I didn't care. I stopped kissing her and unlaced the bloomers at the waist and pulled them down over Natalia's curved hips, running my fingers over the ghostly white cold skin pulled taut over her bones and flat stomach. I wanted to see her pussy, but I didn't know what to do next. I was ridiculously over-come with shyness. We both were. Natalia started to cross her legs, tried to pull my hand away, but the touch triggered the madness all over again. I ripped the bloomers right off and there it was, the awesome blonde triangle of hair, untouched, untrimmed, presumably Carlo liked it that way and so, waxed and plucked as I was, did I.

A manic giggle bubbled in my throat as momentarily I imagined Carlo, maybe his mother too, hell, the other nuns, Father Luca, the gardener, Hazel, the hotel barman, let them all come, bend nearer to see more closely as I pushed my face into Natalia's blonde pubic curls, damp with excitement, edged my nose in between the hidden lips, breathed in the unmistakable sharp tang of aroused female. My own pussy twitched frantically.

Natalia took hold of my head and tugged me away, back up for another kiss. I moved my face back over her stomach, over the rough folds of skirt still pushed up round her waist, back up to her naked breasts, closed my eyes as I rubbed my lips against the hard nipples, and then back to Natalia's mouth, her lovely, warm, wet, open mouth, and kissed her again, pushed my tongue inside because that really felt the best.

As I kissed her, I rubbed myself against her leg. I couldn't help it. My body was tight, coils of desire unwinding with all the sensations, and I couldn't help shoving my hand into the warm space between her milky-white thighs.

Up in the tower the bell tolled.

'Shit. My coda!' Natalia growled, tossing her head from side to side. 'They're summoning me. Oh, lick me, Jenni! Lick my sex. Bring me back to life!'

'Calm down, Sister! I'll do better than that. I'll lick you till you're begging me to stop!'

I giggled softly, but anxiety pricked at me as the bell echoed round the neighbouring buildings. Natalia arched her back defiantly and as the wretched coda beat through the air she grabbed my face and pushed me roughly so that I slid back down her stomach, and she opened her legs. I saw the juicy treat opening stickily, curls of hair clinging to keep it concealed, the vivid red promise as her sex lips pulled apart, and I grabbed hold of her red-striped bottom and lifted it to my face like a prize and ran my tongue up the dark-pink crack to lick up that moisture. A ripple of delicious shock ran through me to smell the other woman's female scent, startling my senses with the untried, sweet-salt flavour.

Natalia's sex felt like silk against my face. I was getting drunk on the smell of her. I let my tongue lead me again, sliding it over the slit, feeling Natalia tense up and shiver as I swept my tongue once, twice up over the furls of her sex, feeling the bump of the little clit revealing itself in there. I found myself lapping at Natalia like a cat at her kitten, making the girl twitch and groan with every stroke.

'Please, Jenni. I'm creaming myself here. Lick me, please.' Natalia was moaning and offering herself desperately.

Once more the bell rang.

As my tongue parted the nun's soft lips, probed deeper, past the tender frills inside, it was being sucked into her tight little hole. It was all sweet sweat and honey in there. My fingers hooked into Natalia's buttocks and slithered into the warm crack between her butt cheeks, and my own cunt clenched with mad excitement as I burrowed inside her and Natalia writhed and lifted beneath me, and then my tongue touched the little bump of her clit, and Natalia moaned like a porn star.

Triumph surged through me, I was on it now, and I sucked harder, opening up the lips like petals, and Natalia reared upwards and slammed and thumped against the bed and as she shuddered with her climax I fingered myself quickly and roughly, still licking out my beautiful Natalia, and my cunt gripped tightly as I came, too, then fell away, exhausted.

The bell echoed again.

'Oh, I want to stay here,' I murmured. 'I think I've heard that call. That voice from on high. I know it means no sex. At least not with men, but who cares when I feel horny all the time?'

There was no answer.

I opened my eyes. Natalia was standing by the bed. She was dressed, but something was odd about her appearance.

'I'm going outside, *cara*, but I need you to stay here.' Her voice was harsh in the silence. Then I realised what was odd. She was wearing the black habit I'd brought in to the convent. Not her own grey one.

'Don't fucking *cara* me! What are you playing at, you little –' I scrambled to my knees on the bed, tried to grab at my clothes, but she put her hand up in the same stern way Mother Superior had.

'I mean, I want you to swap places with me. Just for a night.'

'So all that sweetness. That sex –' I gaped at her. 'You've been using me!'

She shook her head. 'It's not like that. I wanted to try it. You made it irresistible. And I meant everything I said. But I need to see Carlo one last time, Jennifer. You said you'd help me. So you stay in here, do my job in the winery, they won't know the difference. Even Sister Antonia says we look alike.'

'Who?'

'She has red hair and freckles. The one who was holding you back last night. She remarked on it when we were all back in our cells.' She came and sat down stiffly in her unaccustomed clothing. I twitched sulkily away. 'Listen. I'll finish with him, and then I'll come back to you.'

'You don't want me. You did all that, just to take advantage.' I slumped on the bed. 'I'm such a bloody fool.'

Natalia stood up. 'By the way, I did fake it, you know.'

Now the tears were hot in my eyes. She leant over me and kissed me in an incredibly wanton, lustful rush, pushing her tongue into my mouth, pulling at my hair. I pushed her off me.

76

'What did you just say?'

'My ankle. Yesterday.' She laughed softly, and opened the door. 'It didn't hurt *that* much. I just wanted you to stay around a little longer!'

Chapter Five

Sister Perpetua plucked a couple of swollen grapes out of their leafy hiding place. Natalia had taken over the convent's wilting, failing mini vineyard last summer when she joined, and after her tender care the vines were already into their second harvest. The bottles from the first were lined up in glinting rows in the cellar, but the first thing my – sorry, Sister Perpetua's – marketing mind noticed when I reported for duty that morning was the atrocious labelling. Someone, Natalia presumably, had merely scrawled *La Religieuse* on luggage tags and strung these round the necks.

The grapes were perfect, though. So ripe in the palm of my hand. God, I was thirsty. The greenhouse was like an oven. And I was hungry, too. Breakfast was a dry roll before daybreak, and we were not allowed to eat again until noon. I could just take one tiny bite before lugging this last basket over to the wine press. My teeth would pierce the translucent skin, biting the red fruity flesh. The juice spurting on to my tongue, the cool, naughty liquid trickling down my throat. No one would ever know ...

Except I would know. I was a nun, even if only temporarily, and I had to obey the rules. I seemed to be growing a conscience like some kind of tumour, without even realising it. How Hazel would laugh, if she read my mind. If she could see me now. But how could she? How indeed could she even know where I was, because I'd stupidly left my bag, my iPad and my phone in Caffe Florian.

But weirdly, I didn't care. Someone would pick them up and take them to the hotel. Or steal them. Whatever. In a couple of days the convent had slowly wound itself around me like swaddling. Even outside sounds here were muffled behind the high wall, so you could be anywhere in the world. The Navajo desert. Ealing Common. The world had no meaning for me now.

Natalia had instructed me to stick to the name Sister Perpetua if I was challenged, but so far they hadn't sussed out the great swap, or noticed Natalia's absence. Then again as no one was allowed to speak, no one had said a word. Not at prayers, not at meals. I had steered well clear of Mother Marta and her sidekicks, but I was sure that Freckles – the scary one who had held me back the other night when Natalia was being flogged – suspected something. Wherever I looked, walked, sat, knelt, she was somewhere near. Watching me. Was it the Rouge Noir, perhaps, showing when I was telling my rosary beads? With no access to nail-varnish remover, by such little details I could yet be discovered and brought to justice if I wasn't very careful.

'Tempting to eat what you can get your hands on when you're out here, far away from prying eyes, isn't it? Just like the Garden of Eden.'

Oh God, it was her. Freckles. Or rather, if I wanted to show due respect and survive this challenge, Sister Antonia. A mindreader as well as second-in-command dominatrix. Swinging her rounded Irish body nimbly through the moist greenery. In my starving state she looked as if she was floating.

I sat very still, my face frozen in what I hoped was a suitably transported expression, hoping she'd think I was in some kind of holy ecstasy. Praying she wouldn't haul me before Mother Marta and have me punished. Flogged. Whipped. And worst of all, thrown out into the cold to explain myself to Hazel, Signora Martelli ...

I groaned inwardly and waited for the blow. But she simply squatted down on the other side of a tray of seedlings, picked up a wine bottle from a stack of crates, and twisted the cork out with her teeth like a navvy.

I glanced at the bell tower. Five minutes before the next silent meal. Christ, how quickly I'd learned to measure out my day in bells, prayers and scraps of food.

'Technically you can converse if you're working,' she continued briskly. 'But I could still have you brought before Mother Superior and royally castigated.' Sister Antonia took a deep swig from the bottle, and handed it to me. 'In fact we constantly patrol the grounds and drag our Sisters before her to be whipped, particularly the new ones, for the slightest of misdemeanours, whether or not they deserve it. And do you know what? They end up thanking us.'

Her sleeve brushed mine, and I actually blushed. Even touching garments was forbidden. Which made every glance, every accidental contact, doubly tantalising. I obediently swallowed the wine, and its potency went straight to my head.

'We all know you're an impostor, Sister Perpetua. Well, not all of us. I admit I've kept it from Her Highness, and from Father Luca. But we could all do with a newcomer, a new playmate, so I don't want to ruin the surprise just yet. I'm saving the big reveal for when Sister Benedicta comes home.'

My throat seemed to have taken the vow of silence.

'Cat got your tongue? Or God got it, perhaps? Let's see if we can get you to speak.' Sister Antonia ran her finger over my top lip. 'Smell that!'

I sniffed her finger, knowing I shouldn't. The sharp, sweet tang on her skin was instantly familiar.

'That's my pussy juice. From this morning.'

'Sister, my God!' I gasped. 'What have you been doing?'

'Silly question!' She slapped at my hand. 'Why, pleasuring myself, of course! You don't think we go through a lifetime of celibacy without at least masturbating? And the special treat was those nice chunky candles our new Sister kindly brought in the other day. You know what they're for, don't you?'

I shrugged. 'Lighting the chapel?'

Freckles leaned forward and slid her hand up under the irritating white linen veil flapping round my shoulders to touch the soft skin on my neck. I shivered.

'Hmm. Been a long time since you had a man, has it, Sister Perpetua? If you respond that quickly to one little touch, how do you think you'll feel back in the big bad world, when you have a real live cock ramming up you? Two gorgeous men fucking you maybe, front and back, both at the same time?' She laughed softly, still stroking my neck, and took another swig from the bottle. 'That was my fantasy this morning, anyway. Just me, and my big fat candle. I mean my *two* big fat candles.'

The words buzzed like bees against my covered ears. My assumed innocence had taken a stronger hold than I'd thought. None of that would particularly have shocked me a week ago. I'd have been reading about it in some chat magazine riding the tube to work with barely a raised eyebrow. But now electrifying sensations shot through me from the place where Sister Antonia was still touching my neck as if I'd never been touched before. Down to my poor neglected pussy, hidden far away under my apron, under my dress, under my serge petticoat, under the scratchy bloomers where I could feel it responding. Naked, warm, loosening. She was gorgeous, actually, now I looked at her more closely. Brazen and full on, physically pretty tough, but yes, that freckly skin like butterscotch, the full lips and the wicked glint in her copper-coloured eyes could easily bring a grown man to his knees. I was already so into my part as quiet little Sister Perpetua, and she was so overbearing, so confident in these strange surroundings.

'Shall I tell you what else you're missing, Sister? All those earthly delights you've left behind? The ones that little tart Sister Benedicta is tasting right this minute? That she'll never want to give up? You know she'll never come back, don't you? Already she's stayed out longer than she promised. You're in here for ever.' She tilted her head in typical nun-like fashion and her wide mouth spread in a dirty grin. 'Well, hush my mouth. Lucky old us.'

I didn't know whether to laugh or cry. The wine was making me feel so mellow, so relaxed, that the thought of being in here, staying in here, was not only attractive, it was becoming essential. My final lifestyle choice.

'Don't you ever stop talking?'

We both glanced up at the clock. One minute to go.

'Depends how badly I want to be punished.' Sister Antonia chuckled, licking wine off her lower lip. 'Just enjoy teasing myself, teasing you, teasing anyone who'll listen. Think of what Sister Benedicta's lover is doing to her now. Kissing, licking, his cock going hard when she strokes it. The feel of it sliding in, opening you up, pushing inside you.'

I shuddered. 'Why are you in here, for God's sake, if all you want is a good fuck?'

And then the bell started to ring from the tower. We both glanced up to watch it swinging heavily from its wooden frame.

'Oh, I have everything I need. Right here.' Freckles jumped up, looked down at me. 'See you later, Sister. I'll leave you to your precious vines.'

We smiled at each other, and again there was that fluttering of unease from my newly sprouted conscience. If I was attracted to Sister Antonia, that was deceiving my Natalia. But then again, who the hell was Natalia anyway? Certainly not mine. I owed her nothing, and she owed me everything. So if Freckles, another sexy, beautiful woman, was here for the taking, what, or who, was stopping me?

Sister Antonia even moved differently as she headed back out into the garden. Not the ghostly glide they all normally adopted, but a more obstinate stride. I couldn't keep my eyes off her. The way she moved showed her body, her hips, the secret curve of her breasts. Her habit even dipped into the divide between her legs as she walked. It was as if I could see right through her clothes to those long legs. Did she have a red bush, to go with that colouring?

The last basket of grapes was heavy, but I kept silent as I lifted, thinking naughty thoughts about Sister Antonia's flame-coloured pussy, her strong fingers parting the lips to let me see the red slash inside ...

I didn't even grunt as I carried the basket towards the cool press ready to be turned into intoxicating wine. Someone was rolling barrels about in the wine house while the augur fed the grapes into the crusher, but no one else was visible. They would all be inside, scrubbing the floors or preparing lunch. Meanwhile I was far better off out here. Starving, half-cut, and fantasising about another woman!

I staggered across the dusty garden with the basket, then stopped. One of my stockings had come loose, was rolling down my leg and irritating me, the black wool scratching my skin, which was raw and sensitive as if I'd been burned. Everything about this place put me on high alert. I pointed my toe like a ballerina, lifted my skirt and reached under it to yank up the stocking.

A bird screeched up and I jumped round, leg still

cocked. The enormous gardener was there, holding my basket. He turned, and started walking off towards the wine press. I got a better look at him. Tangled black hair and wide shoulders and long legs in baggy blue trousers. Strong brown arms, the muscles flexing as he lifted my heavy basket like it was a punnet of strawberries.

My stomach knotted. I let the skirt drop down, and again felt suffocated instead of comforted. Would I ever get used to this get-up? I wanted to kick it all off, the skirt, the veil, feel the cold air on my skin.

'What do we do next? With the grapes?'

He didn't answer. Of course. He was deaf. I tapped him on the shoulder and he looked round slowly. Oh, Lordy, I had a really good look at him this time and talk about a bit of rough. Wild, unshaven, dirty. And apparently furious. He didn't catch my eye, or speak. He stared, hard, at my mouth. My hands clenched under my gardening apron, pressing right into my lap. My lips felt hot and swollen, the way he stared. I could hear the breath rushing through, see the pulse pounding in his powerful neck.

The bell tolled again, and when his eyes flicked sideways it was like a match blowing out. I dithered, wondering if it was time for me to go inside. It wasn't my coda, but no one had told me what to do. He turned towards the wine press, so I followed him. His arms were so strong, the muscles flexing under the skin. It started to rain. Not the usual insidious Venetian rain, but a real downpour. We both ran across the garden into the press, and the rain thundered down on the cheap tin roof. The gardener dumped the basket and bent down beside a barrel, turned the tap and studied the dark-red liquid pouring into a big jug. The sweet potent aroma made me feel even more pissed.

I arched my back, aching from bending over those vines. The rain had curled his black hair on his neck, stuck his wet shirt to his spine and ribs.

Silently he turned the tap off and squatted there on the dusty floor, sniffing the liqueur expertly before taking a swig.

I was soaked through, and trembled as I went to stand in front of him. It was so easy not speaking. Seductive, even. Why do we all make so much noise? The gardener swilled the liquid round his mouth, staring calmly up at me, then swallowed. A drop of rain was elongating at the end of one curl, ready to fall on to his forehead. It was unusually warm in here. The silence and the still falling rain hummed in my ears.

He studied my knees, which were on a level with his face, then his gaze ran up my legs, rested briefly on my lap, my fiddling, kneading fingers, then up over my bound chest to my face, which started to go red.

'I'm here to help you,' I croaked, and coughed. He waited, staring, again, at my mouth. I touched my lips, and they still felt as if they were burning. 'But I've never done this before. This convent lark. This silence. But I guess you're used to it!'

Laughter slid dangerously around inside me, and I waved my hand. My sleeve brushed his hair. He jerked his head.

'Would you like to see my ideas for the wine labels? These really won't do. Not for the commercial market.'

He started smiling. He had beautiful, even, white teeth. His stubble seemed to be growing darker and thicker as I looked at him.

'You know I'm not really Sister Benedicta, don't you? Don't care who knows it, frankly. I'm Sister Perpetua. The new girl.' I took some labels out of my pocket. 'The design hasn't been approved by Mother Mary or Sister Agnes or any of the other seniors yet, and I hope Natalia – Sister Benedicta – won't mind.'

I'd drawn the outline of a nun from the back, curvacious in a ridiculously tight-fitting habit, reaching up to pluck a grape. He glanced at the image, then back at me.

He stood up and came very close, paused a moment. Waiting, maybe, for me to move away. But I didn't. I couldn't. I could feel the wall of warmth between us. The way he stared at my mouth as if he wanted to eat it. Then he lifted his hands and I held my breath. But he didn't touch me. Instead he sketched my hidden curves with his big hands, tracing the same shape as my design, and buried beneath the ugly bandages my nipples hardened and tingled in response.

Still the rain drummed on the roof. The drop fell off his hair on to his nose. My veil was weighted with water. The guy took the hem, squeezed water out of it. Heat radiated out of him, even at arm's length. I tried hard to remain calm and nun-like, but this was a son of the soil all right because as he stared again at my mouth he yanked my veil and the white cap right off and as I screeched and tried to grab them back he held them up disdainfully.

'Hey, *signor*, you can't do that – give them back to me!'

He sniggered and tossed the pathetic piece of cloth into the dark corner, behind the barrels. Slowly I put my hands up to ruffle out my hair. Now he'd know I wasn't a real nun, but God, how good that felt. He came up and took hold of both my wrists in one hand, wound a strand of tangled hair round the finger of the other hand and rubbed it under his nose as if it was a herb or a petal. I melted at the incredible sexiness of the gesture. No wonder they cut the hair off those poor girls. It was their crowning glory and this guy was starved of pleasure just as they were.

I could see my reflection in each of his dark eyes, two miniature Jennifers.

His hands started to slide down my neck, just where Sister Antonia had touched me. He lifted the wet collar away from my clammy skin, and touched where my pulse was hammering. Sparks of electricity seemed to crackle off me. He stared at my throat, down at my apron and the rough blouse underneath it. Obviously with no hearing his other senses were all the stronger. The thought of those senses made me even weaker.

The rush through the rain had made the rough linen cling to my torso. The man smiled slowly and instinctively I pushed my shoulders back to thrust my breasts out.

His fingers moved round to flick open the top button. 'We need to do the bottling.' I tried feebly to pull away. 'They'll check.'

He took his hands away and picked up the jug. Shit. He'd taken my warning literally. No more fondling. No chance of a wicked shag in the wine house. But then he pushed the jug against my mouth and tilted it until I was forced to drink. The wine was so strong, so delicious. The way he was tipping it, some spilt down my chin, trickled on to my skin where he'd opened the button. I wiped my mouth, giggling quietly, and felt the alcoholic haze spreading through me all over again. He smiled and took another big gulp. Now his lips were red, and wet with wine.

Shards of excitement jabbed at me. I was desperate for another touch, inwardly clamouring to feel one flick of his fingertips again. He was so close I could count every bristle pushing through the dark skin on his chin.

He started to massage my shoulders so that I was forced to relax. My neck went limp. He undid the next button. And the next. Not easy. They were tiny buttons. A little thought darted into my head. Was he practised at this? It jolted me, and I tried to cover myself, because the buttons were undone to my waist now and I didn't want him to see how repulsive those bound breasts looked. Sure enough, he stopped.

'That's right. We must stop.' I shook my head, started to do up the buttons, but he ripped open the blouse, and started to cut, with his shears, at the bandages underneath. 'How am I going to bind myself up again now?'

But we both shrugged at each other. Why the hell was I worrying about stuff like that? I wasn't a real nun. Was I?

But I was shivering like a virgin in front of him. My knees buckled. I did nothing to help him. Stood there like a little doll. A pulse throbbed deep between my legs. My sensitive breasts tightened and started to swell, rising up triumphantly like dough as the bandages loosened, cut into shreds, and dropped to the floor. Now they were offered, pale and soft in the shadows. My nipples hardened, dark and red. The man pushed my shirt off my shoulders and traced the ridge of my collarbone, treading his finger tips across the exposed skin and under the shirt again, slowly towards my breasts, and I pushed them brazenly towards him, my breath coming in uneven gasps of longing.

His features became blurred and fused. I closed my eyes, let my head droop backwards as the wine and this man's surprisingly tender caresses lulled me. He came closer. I could feel his breath hot on my skin. I moved my head so that his mouth bumped up against mine. My breath stopped totally then. I couldn't move. My lips softened and parted. He rubbed his mouth against my lips. I slid my hands up his back and there was a quiver between his shoulder blades.

I pressed harder. I was as desperate to touch as to be touched. He flicked the tip of his tongue against my teeth, and then around the inside of my lips, and he tasted of wine but more than that he was masculine, male, strong, salty, sweet, wet, warm. I pushed my tongue inside his mouth and he trapped it, sucking it in between his teeth, so that my face was moulded into his and my body was pressed against the length of him.

I thought he was murmuring something, but that was impossible. He pulled his shirt off as we kissed then with no further ado he reached down and lifted up my skirt.

What was left of my pretend sanctity struggled up and I battered weakly at his chest. 'No, I can't. We have to work. The bell will go soon and we have done nothing!'

But he interpreted my lack of conviction correctly and lifted me up and dropped me on to an old pile of hessian sacks, some empty, others full of crackling leaves. He was massive against the rainy daylight. We were enclosed in the darkness. Everything suddenly felt wicked, and dangerous. I really felt as if I was about to commit a terrible sin. I thought, as I lay there, that I must look like some kind of sacrifice. The thought made me wriggle frantically despite all efforts to remain still.

He reached behind him to grab two bottles out of a crate. He grinned as he ripped a label off my roll of new ones, swiped one across his wet tongue, and stuck it onto the elegant green glass flank. Then he banged in a cork and flourished it back into the crate before spreading out his hands triumphantly.

'Job done! Christ, you are wicked!' I clapped my hands. 'You must be like a bull in a china shop, all these women, these nuns, and you the only man!'

He laughed then, a kind of husky breath, filled up the other bottle and tipped some more into my laughing mouth. This time it splashed all over my breasts, dripped on to my nipples, and we stopped laughing. My dark-red nipples were wet with wine. He remained kneeling. I reached up, and pulled him down on top of me. The rough sacking scratched where my blouse had ridden up. I raised my spine to escape the prickles, arching my breasts towards his hands, his mouth.

'They told me never to speak to you,' I whispered. 'But they didn't tell me not to touch you.'

93

He nodded as if he'd heard me, and the warmth inside me flared into fire. Who needs words, anyway? His nostrils were flared with the effort of breathing calmly. He was straddling me now, heavy on my legs. My breath was shallow, barely there. He held my arms above my head with one hand while the other moved to my breast, felt its weight. Then he bent down, muscles bulging in his arm as he supported his weight, and sucked the wine off my nipple.

I moaned loudly. Oh, yes, this was everything a girl could need. No words, no hassle, no grief. Just hot, hard gratitude.

He put one knee between my legs, still sucking, opening me, then he lifted my skirt, petticoat, getting to the cumbersome bloomers. I squirmed with confusion, tried to cover the horrible undergarments, but he ducked his head under my skirt to take a good look, the greed and lust in his face making me wriggle even more. Then he pushed the skirt and petticoat up to my waist, cold air playing across my thighs. He yanked the bloomers down. The slight ripping sound was electrifying in its quiet violence.

So I opened my legs for him as he touched me, right there, in my ready, wet crack.

Through the thin material of his trousers I could feel the thick outline of his cock jabbing at my thigh, nudging against the cleft at the top. The rain rushed through the door like sudden, hushed voices.

I was getting frantic now. I wrenched my hands free and took hold of his hips, pulling him up a little so that I could unbuckle his belt. I tore at his jeans. I wanted him inside me, his cock pushing up and fucking me. Oh yeah. A real man at last. All the girls in all the world could never equal the ecstasy of feeling warm strong hands, a forceful mouth and a big stiff cock. Could they?

He grabbed my wrists and forced them again over my head and this time I was well and truly pinned down while he drew his cock out and let it nudge in between my legs. Forget nudging. I wanted it in there. Now. I wound my legs round him and pulled him in to me. By now he must have realised, if there was ever any question, that I was no more a virgin than Madonna.

The hay scratched into the crack of my bottom. His eyes burned as he paused inexplicably. He was staring at my mouth again.

'Yes,' I growled. 'Read my lips, lover. Fuck me.'

God, how dirty, how horny, how funny this all was! Fucking in a cold, wet, silent convent garden, far hornier than the plushest of hotels or the sunniest of beaches! An explosive rush of excitement spurted through me, crazy and hot. I was lost. Any more words were stopped by moans of pleasure as he started to run his cock up the soft skin of my inner thighs, guiding it to my swollen wet pussy. I wriggled to get it deeper inside, gripping to take in the warm, throbbing length. No niceties, no teasing, now, just get on and get in and up and faster and as it slid inside I gripped him to keep the fire tight inside and felt the gathering pleasure darken to a hot peak ready to shatter me. No waiting. No possibility of waiting.

He slid the head of his cock along the tender groove then thrust his cock right in, really hard, until his balls banged against me. Then he thrust again, and again, scraping me against the sacking, lifting me with the violence of it. Vaguely I wondered why he was so hard, so urgent. Had he really not had sex, like me, for ages? Had none of those nuns succumbed to him? Was I the first? Were they all mouth and no knickers? Was I really blazing a trail here?

My thoughts were obliterated by my own shrieks of pleasure. He crushed me as he fucked me, all that male heaviness and heat on me, then he shuddered violently, kissing and biting my mouth as the excitement burst inside me, too, split my willing not so virginal body wide, wide open.

'If this is the Garden of Eden, then you're my Adam,' I chuckled lazily, when I'd got my breath. 'How about we bottle *you*?'

He twined a strand of hair round his finger and pulled my head towards his. I smiled and went on smiling, even when the bell started tolling and I could swear I heard those voices again, a rustling, a snapping of skirts, a scudding of feet away across the wet grass.

'The way you watch my mouth all the time,' I said, easing my hand down to touch his warm cock. It started to lift and nudge against my palm like an animal. 'That's because you're reading my lips?'

'No.' His voice was baritone deep, gruff and totally shocking. 'It's because next time I want you to wrap them around my cock.'

* * *

'Well done, playmate. You were worth every penny.'

My eyes sprang open. Sister Antonia was standing in the doorway of my cell. All the doors had been removed, which I later learned was one of the many punishments imposed on the majority for the sins of the few.

'Penny?'

She came further into the room. She was wearing the long linen nightgown which all the nuns wore at night-time, and was carrying, yes, a long, thick candle which, with one of mine, cast the only light in the room.

'Well, not pennies exactly. We use communion wafers. Serious penalties from Father Luca if we're found stealing those, but they are very handy currency, I can tell you. Anyway we had bets on you fucking the gardener today. Those bells you heard were calling us out for our outdoor exercise. God knows we needed something entertaining to watch!'

'So glad to be of service,' I murmured weakly.

'Some of us were pretty hard-core gal-pals when we came in here,' she remarked thoughtfully, one bare foot scratching the other. I noticed on her bare ankle an angel tattoo. 'But now you've broken in young Zippo, I think we can give him a whirl. The silent stud. How about that!'

So they hadn't heard him speaking.

She turned to go. 'I do hope you'll stay around, Sister.'

Her light went flickering away down the corridor, throwing up Gormenghast-type shadows, and I was left shivering with my thoughts. And with my candles. My fingers strayed under my nightgown. What an amazing day. Two days. There was astonishment round every corner. You'd think that there'd be nothing else to discover after a week or two, but somehow I reckoned there was much, much more to this convent than met the eye.

And instead of reducing my reawakened sexual urges, being in here made them stronger, more urgent than ever. I pushed up my nightgown. My nails scratched over the cool white flesh of my thighs, sensed the warmth pulsating from my opening sex, yearned to go in further.

Down the hall Sister Antonia and the other Sisters slept. Or perhaps they didn't? Perhaps after they'd all watched me and the gardener humping in the wine press, they all lay there dreaming of us or of their past lives full of lovers, remembering naked limbs and bodies rubbing against each other and getting sweaty, men kissing and touching, maybe even other women kissing and touching them. My Sisters, putting fingers inside themselves while they writhed silently on their unforgiving horsehair pallets. And thought of me.

There was the sweet moisture springing in the one or two tiny hairs growing back on my pussy. There was the pulse, going thickly and strongly, just inside, close enough to touch, still sore from Natalia's fingers, sorer still from the gardener's cock. It was a delicious pain, though. And I wanted more.

I picked up a candle from the box beside my bed, making the others roll and rattle loudly. I felt its smooth, waxy length, the width, the strength which would easily take a bit of a battering, oh, and just right for slipping inside ... The clatter of the candles must have woken them, because a couple of doors down someone moaned. Someone else sighed. Just quickly, what would be the harm, why not tiptoe down the passage and see what they were doing?

It was the same in each little cell, the cells with no doors. One or two girls were asleep, like effigies, stretched serenely with their hands crossed over their chests. But the others? Wow. There was Sister Frances flinging her head from side to side, her knees bent up and falling open as she plunged her candle in and out of her cunt in a rapid wanking movement, ready to come. Next door Sister Lucia was taking it slowly, only just starting to arch her back up off the bed with each slow thrust. And in her slightly bigger cell at the far end, Sister Antonia was on all fours, head buried in the pillow, while one hand fucked herself with the candle, the other played with her cunt, rubbing frantically in counterpoint to the determined push of the candle.

I dashed back down the corridor, past all my groaning, writhing Sisters. I couldn't wait to get into my hard little horsehair pallet. I lay down, kicked the fraying sheet off me, tickled the tip of the candle on to the soft, already twitching skin, pushed it through the swelling sex lips to be slicked in wetness, eased it inside, oh so gently, back and forth in a little rocking rhythm, careful not to hurt, opening my knees wider to feel its brutal length, felt a scream bunching up as I pulled it back, in again, touched the bud, flares of excitement gripping, burning so hard –

And just then a loud voice, Mother Superior's voice, barked, somewhere in the shadows at the far end of the corridor: 'Candles out now, girls!'

Chapter Six

There were some intense glances from the Sisters when I came in from the garden for lunch the next day. Eyes lit up even more when they saw I was carrying several bottles of wine. Amazing how silence can ripple, how you can almost touch it. Eyes followed me up and down the refectory as I poured out glasses of wine, Sisters raising chunky tumblers brimming with that ruby liquid with only one question on their lips.

Had I done it again with Zippo the gardener?

They were trying to sense it, smell it off me as I lined the bottles up on the sideboard, new labels prominent, then collected my bowl of soup and sat down on the hard wooden bench to eat. I enjoyed it. Yes, of course I enjoyed it. The attention. The quiet shuffling in chapel, in the kitchen shelling peas, in the scullery scrubbing pans, to get closer to me, the unspoken desire of the Sisters to speak to me if they could find a way. Find out more about me and my world. And what I'd done with Zippo the gardener.

I winced as the soup burnt my mouth. The same mouth that had, as instructed, wrapped itself round his erect cock not an hour since. Even so, it was they who had so much to teach me, I reckoned, looking round at those pale, solemn faces shrouded in their veils. How they existed inside these walls, contemplating poverty, chastity and obedience, and silence, for ever, all the while retaining their wide-eyed, enthusiastic innocence.

I caught Sister Antonia's eye from the far side of the room. She seemed to be trying to tell me something. Warn me? And beside her Sister Frances, too, was making the sign of the cross and tilting her head towards the chapel.

I started to smile at them both, warm in my new popularity, when the bubble abruptly burst. The double doors opened to reveal Mother Superior. I stifled a smile. Honestly. She should be on the stage. It was like something out of *The X Factor*. All it needed was the shiny floor, the smoke, hysterical applause.

She glared around the refectory then crooked her forefinger at me. 'Sister Benedicta. Confession. Now.'

I walked slowly towards her, ramrod-straight, picking up my feet, ignoring that ripple of interest from the Sisters as I arranged my face into the requisite pious expression. Only as I reached her did I realise that Mother had called me Benedicta, not Perpetua. So the swap secret was still safe.

Or was it? This was the first time I'd been up close to her since donning Natalia's habit, and her eyes narrowed. I bowed my head quickly so she couldn't detect the obvious differences. Like the fact that I was a good ten years older than Natalia and probably half a stone heavier ...

She swivelled like a robot and processed stiffly up the chilly cloister. The wind was slicing in horizontally today, even though we were surrounded by high walls. Boy, had I been glad to shelter in the warm greenhouse at dawn this morning. And even gladder to feel Zippo's strong, soil-blackened fingers lifting up my heavy skirt and warming the skin on my thighs, sullying them with streaks of earth as he slowly opened them.

She directed me to the chapel and stood aside to let me walk through. 'Father Luca is waiting.'

'Forgive me, Mother, but what have I –?'

'Not for me to forgive.' Her lips snapped shut like a trap and so did the chapel doors.

The confessional was like an upturned coffin, a huge black Tardis lurking in its own little cloister next to the sacristy. I'd seen other Sisters go in there at all times of day and night, but so far I had not felt the need. What did I have to confess? I'd made no vows. I'd be out of here soon, even though this was my fourth morning and there was no sign of Natalia.

The chapel was empty and silent. Watery sun filtered through the stained-glass window above the altar, lighting the dusty pews and stalls. One ray of light pointed like a finger at the confessional, where the little door was creaking open all by itself. I sat down on a kind of shelf and peered at the metal grille. No one there. I waited. It was a relief, actually. Sitting here on my own, away from the Sisters, away from Zippo. I was aching, and tired. A spot of confession might be quite therapeutic.

A tall figure appeared behind the grille and bent its head in prayer.

'Bless me, Father, for I have –' I knew what came next, but I was damned if I was going to say it. And anyway I couldn't speak. The dust motes in there had swirled straight into my lungs. Didn't anyone give this thing a good wipe round?

'Sinned?'

The figure straightened abruptly. His voice behind the grille was clipped, stern and Germanic, not sultry, musical and Italian at all. I felt a sour rush of unreasonable disappointment.

'No. Not bloody sinned,' I wheezed. 'I'm not even supposed to be here.'

'Sister! For that kind of language the penance will already be high!'

I started to cough again, my fury dissolving into choking splutters. The whole confessional shook. My eyes were streaming, I couldn't breathe. I wondered how long I was supposed to stay in here talking to an invisible priest. But he wasn't invisible, because here he was, opening the coffin door.

'I can hear your sins better in the sacristy, Sister.'

I stumbled after him, still wheezing and coughing. Behind the confessional was his inner sanctum, a high-ceilinged, wood-panelled room lit by another huge stained-glass window and filled with huge silver candle-sticks, chalices, vestments and robes and of course the requisite gigantic crucifix. It smelt gorgeous in there. French polish, wine, for some reason that glorious shoe-shop smell of leather, and fresh coffee.

He went and sat on a kind of throne upholstered in purple velvet, motioning with a long white hand for me to sit on a footstool beside him. The light behind him dazzled me a little. At mass and prayers I had only seen him in white robes through clouds of incense, but now he was wearing a simple black cassock. The priestly undergarment beneath all that flamboyance. Thirty-three tiny black buttons marched down the front, representing Christ's years. Five buttons on each sleeve, representing His wounds. A big silver cross rested on his chest.

As I gulped down some water he leaned back and crossed one leg over the other, so that I could see the tensing of his stomach and the working of his muscles, the flexing of his knees, the swinging of his ankle in a perfectly smooth sock above a highly polished shoe.

The silence between us was almost spiritual. Neither of us was in any hurry. Outside, branches scratched at the window. I tried to remember when I had last sat so still, with no phone ringing, no client badgering, no train or plane to catch, no deadline. London, Hazel, all so far away. Another planet ...

A bell started tolling, such a familiar sound to me now. It was the coda for Sister Agnes. Or was it for special chores? But the peace in here was mesmerising.

And so was Father Luca. I stared at his face, now that I was used to the light. He really was like a Bond villain. Cropped hair, steely grey eyes and an angry jaw. Speckles of silvery bristles. Mother Superior must have surprised him, dragged him out of his quarters to hear my evil confession before he'd had a chance to shave. I lowered my eyes to rove over the long black coat, encasing his torso like a glove, the way it clung to his flat stomach, smoothed over the suppressed swell in his groin, flowed to his feet. Like a soldier's mess kit, it would make the plainest of men look glamorous.

My eyes were dragged back to his groin, even though his hands were folded over it now. What demon did he have hidden under there? He, it, was sacred. Untouchable. A slow warmth seeped through my veins like liquid aphrodisiac. Or speed. My heart jolted, and started to pound a little faster. I sat up a little straighter on the uncomfortable stool and thought what to say, how to keep us both here. How to elongate the moment.

Here was a man, an extremely handsome man, surrounded by Sisters forbidden to sin. What would it take to unleash his human side?

'Why did Mother send you to me?'

Because she knows I seem to be permanently horny these days?

'Because of all the deception, Father. I lied to come in here. Sort of. And I've sinned within these walls.'

He dipped his head as if I'd just propounded a scientific theory, rested one finger on his chin.

'God will never forgive me!'

It came out more passionately than I intended, but somehow I meant it. I pressed my face into my hands.

'Go on, Sister. He will forgive you, but only if you confess what you have done to me.'

I shook my head and moaned a little. 'The sin is too terrible.'

He squeezed my shoulder. Honestly, it was like an electric shock. I gasped and looked up at him, my mouth open, and he was staring intently at me. He took his hand away, but gently, stroking it across my back before returning it to his lap.

'The sin, Sister.' He cleared his throat. 'Tell me.'

'Where do I start?' I shook my head as if struggling with devilish voices. 'I'm not a virgin, Father. I love it here, but I don't belong. Sinful thoughts plague me, day and night. And I don't leave it there. I act on them. I have done sinful things.'

To echo my words I punched at his thigh, as if to demonstrate those same wicked actions. The muscle under the black cloth was rock hard. My fingers fell open, waiting for him to repulse me, but he didn't. I rested my hand on his leg, lightly at first, while I watched, under cover of some residual sighing, that place under his robe which I was determined to rouse.

'The sinful things, Sister. You must unburden yourself before I can give you penance.'

I looked up at him and bit my lip, harder than I meant to. I could taste blood. His hand came down over mine, where it rested on his thigh.

'I have touched myself, Father, at night, with my fingers, to give myself sexual pleasure. And I've done it with the candles. I've encouraged the other Sisters to do the same. To push the candles hard inside our bodies, to fuck ourselves with the candles. All the time wishing they were a man's penis.'

He swallowed and went very pale, and stopped swinging his foot.

I lowered my eyes, lifted them again to let him see the fluttering of my super-long eyelashes.

'And on my first day here I was in a cell with another Sister and she touched me. We kissed, and we undressed each other, and we sucked on each other's breasts and vaginas. We made love and we made each other come.'

He shifted in his chair and turned to face the window so that the harsh light outlined his stony features. His tongue ran across his lower lip, leaving a slick of wetness.

'You made love. So it was an act of love, perhaps, not sin.' His voice was croaky.

'I think I do love her, yes, but that's a sin in itself, isn't it? We're not allowed to have friends in here, let alone favourites, but I'm sure the Sisters are all at it, Father. I mean, I've seen Sister Agnes and Sister Frances, they're always together, side by side, in chapel, in the kitchen, walking in the cloisters –'

'That is a matter for them. But this other Sister. The Sister you – you touched. Why is she not here for confession as well?'

'I don't know where she is! She's run away and left me in here!'

There was a brief silence. He bowed his head. This seemed to be the end of it.

I tried a little harder. 'So I have sinned even more, Father, and touched someone else.'

Our hands were still resting together on his leg. I curled one finger tentatively to grip one of his, and his fingers brushed across the palm of my hand. My pussy twitched, and more heat surged through me.

'Whom have you touched?'

I'd caught him unawares, that was for sure. He uncrossed his legs and brought both feet to the floor, leaning towards me. I could smell the soapy freshness of his skin, see lust flickering alight in his eyes. I flicked my stupid white veil away from my cheek.

'Aren't you supposed to be saying Mass in a minute?'

He took me by the shoulders. 'Whom else have you touched, Sister?'

The breath stopped in my throat when I caught the look in his eyes. They were literally burning. His fingers were digging into me, the pain radiating warmth through my bones.

'The gardener, Father. Zippo.' I beat my hands on his chest, making the silver cross bounce. 'I really think this is the Garden of Eden and I'm Eve, or he's Adam. Maybe he's the snake.'

'He's the man, so he is the one who has led you into temptation.' Father Luca started to shake me, and the movement seemed to wake us both up. 'What did he make you do?'

'I came in here with good intentions, honestly I did, even though I was pretending to be Sister Benedicta, but I couldn't help it. I can't give up my worldly ways. I shouldn't be in here –'

'What exactly did you do with this Zippo?'

I took a deep breath. 'I let him take me. Fuck me, Father. Yesterday, in the wine house when we were working. And this morning I was out there again, and this time he wanted me to suck him off, and I did that, I'm known for it, because I swallow. Then I climbed on top of him, because that's my favourite position, and it was my turn, and I got him hard again and rode him like a cowgirl!'

The silence stretched taut like elastic. Even the bells were hushed. Those words! Why did I use those words? With any luck he hadn't understood.

Father Luca understood all right. He pulled me roughly towards him so that I fell right off my wooden stool and was half kneeling, half swooning in his arms. He started to give me an awkward brotherly, fatherly hug, didn't really know what to do with himself, but as I slipped across his knees he ended up lifting me and now I was pressed hard against his chest, his chin banging against my cheekbone. I curled my arms round him, skin crawling with lust on the outside, the sexy core of me melting with desire deep inside.

'Such a bewitching face. Sex written all over it,' he growled into my cheek. 'The devil really has sent you to try us. Me.'

I made a token effort to wriggle away, but his hands kept me still.

'So what happens now, Father?' I lowered my eyes in shame, sliding my hands up and down his legs distract-edly, as if to push away my sins. The black cloth wrinkled, but he didn't stop me touching him. 'I've had sex, right here in the convent, under your noses! What does the Bible say? I've had carnal knowledge!'

I was hot now, breathing hard, and so was he. The sacristy was suddenly stuffy, even though the trees outside were battering to get in. How had the other Sisters not seen the frustration in this man, every day offering up prayers while in front of him the congregation seethed with thwarted female urges?

'Go on talking, Sister.'

His voice rasped like raw silk on my neck as I bowed my head. My hands had reached the tops of his legs now, and he shifted them very slightly apart.

'And the worst of it is, I loved it, Father. I wanted more. That makes me very bad, doesn't it?' I looked up at his throat, and saw him swallowing hard, several times. I bent forwards, pressed my face against his, let my lips move against his cheek so that I could feel the harsh rub of his bristles. 'Or maybe that makes me very good?'

A great shiver went through him. 'I shouldn't listen to this. I can't be near you any more.'

'Oh, but you have to listen! Mother Superior sent me here to tell you my sins.' I ran my hands up his chest and hooked my fingers into his collar so that he couldn't get away. 'There's no one else I can tell.'

His hands fell from my arms. I stayed where I was, leaning more heavily against him, but kept very still. We could hear the anticipation ticking like a clock between us. His breath was in my ears. My lips, still against his skin, started to caress. Another violent shiver convulsed him from his groin right up his body. His hands landed on my hips. Didn't land. Fell, grappled, grabbed, circled my waist, fanned out to clutch at my buttocks, as if he was fighting for purchase on a cliff.

I reached for the top button of his cassock, took it between my fingertips as delicately as I could. The tiny disc slipped, wet from my sweat as my fingers trembled. My uneven breath was the only movement I couldn't keep under control.

'What is my penance, Father?' I undid the top button and he gave a kind of rasping choke. Christ, this guy really hadn't been near anything female for a very long time. If ever! 'I'll do anything you ask me to do.'

'Not me,' he groaned, leaning his head back against the throne. 'Oh, God.'

I pressed my lips just to the side of his mouth. 'Oh yes, of course. God.'

His chest was heaving as if he had just run a marathon, but all power seemed to have left him. I slipped the next button out of its socket. He didn't move. His hands were rigid on the cheeks of my butt. I kept on unbuttoning, staring up at him, and he looked at my mouth. I ran my tongue over both lips.

In the chapel on the other side of the panelled wall someone struck a note on the organ. We both jumped like scalded cats, but towards each other. Our mouths met, paused, his lips felt warm and wet, unyielding at first, frozen with fear probably, but then our mouths were drawn magnetically until they were pressed hard against each other, pushing, pressing, opening now, his tongue first, flicking out – oh, he was the snake! – and licking across my mouth, my teeth, pushing inside, curling round my tongue, pulling it for him to suck, licking, then nibbling, now biting. How can it be that the speaking part of your face, when silent, can send such fiery currents shooting through the rest of your body, sparking in your nipples so that they harden into nuts, searing down your belly until your fanny starts clenching like a furious fist?

And how can it be that a man vowed to chastity was the best kisser I've ever had?

I kicked the stool away. It fell with a clatter. We froze, wondering if anyone in the chapel had heard, but the organ was playing softly now, just the bass notes throbbing through the wall, and now Father Luca came properly to life, yanked me roughly on to his lap, spreading my legs to grip around his as he pulled feverishly at my dress, pulling it up my thighs, pulling impatiently at the bloomers but they were so loose they almost floated off me and there, beneath, I was naked other than the few golden hairs on my pussy. The rough serge fabric of his cassock scraped my crack with a delicious friction. His strong white hands were cool, kneading my bottom as he bumped me fiercely against him. Soon he would feel the dampness, dribbling out of me, right through the dark fabric still covering him.

'Kiss me, Father!'

I held his face and kissed him again. Already the taste of his mouth was familiar, and this time there was no hesitation. His long, strong tongue probed forcefully, and it was my turn to groan because now his fingers were pushing inside my bottom, opening me, barging inside. My groaning echoed off the vaulted ceiling of the sacristy.

'How could something so good be so wrong?' he groaned. 'You are such a witch.'

In answer I gyrated hard against him, and there it was at last, that ridge of stiffness under his cassock, my prize. I started to rub myself back and forth along it, half laughing, undoing some more buttons, delight bubbling up inside me to see his broad chest and his stomach with its line of dark hairs marching south. I smiled, then started to unbutton my grey dress. Time to let the woman out. Time to show him the breasts nestling there, already swollen with desire.

'It's all good, Father.'

I hadn't had time to bandage them up securely after my encounter with Zippo the gardener this morning, so I cradled my breasts so that they nudged out through the top of my dress. I stretched my spine so that the dark-red nipples poked out and were inches from his hungry, wet mouth.

I knelt up on the purple cushion, bent over him, juicy fruit dangling right over his face while I undid the other buttons. He reached up tentatively, ran his fingers over my breasts then took them and squeezed them together, big soft mounds of pure pleasure right there in his face. He closed his eyes, buried his nose between them, sniffed my skin, my sweat, maybe even the smell of earlier sex with the gardener, then suddenly he nipped one raspberry nipple with his teeth and I squealed with shock. It was pure electricity. Zippo hadn't had time to give them the attention they deserved this morning. We were in too much of a rush. I ripped at Father Luca's remaining buttons while he sucked one nipple, his cheeks drawing in with the pull of the suck, and pinched the other until I was nearly going mad with the overwhelming sensations, and then at last my hands were inside his cassock.

I don't know what I expected a priest to wear underneath, but here were silky black trunks and they barely covered his erection. I allowed myself a lingering look at it, so near, so near now. I pulled the shorts down a little way and his cock flung itself upright, quivering as if a wind was buffeting it. My body shivered to see it. But a crazed part of me still wanted to tease, torment, us both. I wriggled backwards, popping my tits out of his mouth, so that I could bend down, ready to lick the beading tip.

'This is how Zippo likes it,' I crooned.

I sucked hard, drawing the rounded head past my teeth, and Father Luca fell back in his chair, totally powerless. In the chapel they were singing now. His cock was hot and heavy in my hand, bulging big and swollen in my mouth. I wanted this to be the first, possibly last, decent blow job he would ever experience. As I sucked, his fingers came back to life, wandering over every dip and curve, exploring every crack and crevice he could reach. The pressure was becoming explosive.

'You truly are a she-devil,' he groaned, but I just laughed, and sucked harder, running my tongue up and down his length, and just as I could feel his body tighten, I pushed the cock out of my mouth and straddled him once again, hushed his mouth with my finger, keeping his length firm and hard in the other hand.

'But you're the one with the horn.' I laughed softly in his ear as I brushed the bulging tip against my ready wetness.

Father Luca's eyes closed again. For a terrible moment I thought he was going to push me off him, but not even *he* was superhuman enough to resist me now we'd come so far. I had him trapped. I rocked very slightly in a little dance while he sprawled helplessly beneath me on his throne, long limbs, white stomach, thumping great cock, fingers inching towards my cunt and creeping inside my butt crack. I teased him a little more, preparing, tipping myself to guide him up, up, sliding him in between the sensitive surfaces. That thick shaft was already wet from where I'd licked it. Now I wanted to slick it with my honey.

Not so helpless after all. Suddenly he grabbed my hips and plunged me downwards. I squealed as the full length of him rocketed up inside me, stolen inches of pure pulsating pleasure. I paused, hard nipples nudging at his face again. He opened his eyes, and they sparked with life as he took one nipple into his mouth again and bit hard on it, and just as he did so he jammed one finger up my arsehole, the dirty man, and made me jerk right off his knee with the delighted shock of it.

He was a real man at last. A man who wanted to fuck me.

I started to stroke, up, down, his finger up my arse following me, sending totally new, firecracker sensations through me. I had no choice but to move with his cock, with his finger, with his mouth and teeth on my tits, engulf him, every filling inch of him grazing every screaming inch of me so that I could only go so far before slamming back down, and each time we met I was wetter and he was harder than ever.

We crashed against each other, over and over, in our sweet rhythm. Fire streaked through me, my breasts pushed at him frantically, his cold eyes watched me and then it started, the ecstasy rolling over me, I was arching to hold the sensation, trying as well to curb the inevitable, but it was shattering on its peak and flooding through me. Father Luca's eyes were still on me as my body bucked and writhed and he smiled slowly then pumped everything he had into me, throwing me upwards with the force of it.

I bit my lips to stop me screaming out loud, while next door the singing grew to a crescendo. I wondered what on earth they were doing in chapel at this time, with Father Luca in here instead of out there on the altar, what particular service was going on in there, but still we rocked together, thrusting and panting like we were fighting, his robe open to reveal that sacred, magnificent body, buttons scattered like sins, my virginal dress unbuttoned, and then the keys of the organ banged down for the final chord and we shuddered and exploded together.

Father Luca smoothed back a strand of hair that had escaped from the veil I still wore, buttoned my dress briskly and extremely expertly, and stood up. He had turned back into a priest. Just like that. He started to do up what buttons were left on his cassock.

'This can never happen again.'

'You don't mean that.' I stood up, too, and pushed

his hands away so I could do his buttons for him. He swayed slightly. I throbbed and ached, but the man who had fucked me had already evaporated. I got down on my knees. 'You need to give me my penance.'

Father Michael wiped his face with a pure white cloth hanging on a rail. I wondered if it would leave his image there. Then he opened the door to the chapel, which meant that our conversation was finished. He looked at me and smiled for the first time. He really was like Dracula.

'Oh, Sister Perpetua, I think you should be rewarded for that performance. It is I who should be seeking punishment.'

Chapter Seven

I should have been praying, down on my knees in front of the plain cross nailed to my wall. But I had crashed out on the bed. Well, I'd had five long days of hard graft in the garden, barely eating, barely sleeping, and shagging two men from both ends of the spectrum more times than I'd had hot meals in the last few years, not to mention starting to get attention from my eager, curious Sisters – what did you expect? I was absolutely knackered.

The only thing that had been getting and keeping me awake the last two mornings was the little whip Sister Antonia had given me after my 'confession' with Father Luca.

'You know what you've been doing,' she said to me

that night, as I blearily pulled my thick nightgown over my head. 'We all know. There are grilles all over this convent, so we can always spy on each other. So we, and Mother, always know when our Sisters are being good, and when they are sinning.'

I laughed at her. Who needed grilles and spy holes, anyway? We still had no doors on our cells, so there was nothing to knock on. No privacy whatsoever. All the Sisters glided silently from room to room without so much as a by-your-leave. And far from making us all better behaved, it seemed to evaporate any inhibitions altogether. I didn't know if this was a new thing or not, but I had walked past Sister Frances' cell an hour or so earlier and seen her on her bed, thrusting her candle hard and fast in and out of her pussy, while kneeling over her was Sister Agnes, her nightgown hitched right up over her hips, holding on to the iron bedstead and lowering herself, very slowly, on to Sister Frances' face.

'Sister Perpetua, I am speaking to you!' Sister Antonia stepped closer. I pulled my white cap more tightly over my hair and smiled at her to disarm her. She hesitated, and smiled back.

'You have a dimple when you smile, Sister.' I stroked my finger into the dent in her cheek. 'It's very cute. Makes you look softer.'

She tossed her head, colour flaring in her cheeks. 'For as long as you are here with us, you are to use this daily, whenever you are alone in your cell reflecting on your sins.' She handed me this tiny switch. 'If you are not sure what to do with it, the Sisters will show you.'

'Oh, I've already observed them, Sister.'

I had patrolled the corridor at the requisite time of dawn, and seen them. Flagellating. I remembered Natalia talking about flagellating to get her impure thoughts of me out of her head, but this looked much more like pleasure than punishment. The Sisters would pull down their nightgowns over their shoulders and flick the switch across their bare skin, but although there was a suitably sickening thwack against their tender flesh, the moans which followed each slap, the sensuous tilting back of their heads, the licking of their lips and the bellydance of delight they sketched in their bare feet after each one were positively sexual in their response.

'But I've never done it myself. Will you show me, Sister?'

I turned my back and pulled my nightgown over my shoulder without waiting for her reply. There was a pause, and then I heard her take a step back, take a breath inwards, then there was a swish of sliced air before the thing struck me on my shoulder blade. I smacked my hand over my mouth to stop the gasp of pain. I could feel the vicious red line cutting across my skin, like a line of fire branded into me, but after a few moments I felt the sharp sting diffusing into intense, invigorating heat spreading through me.

'Always strike yourself on your back, Sister. In any case it's the only place you can reach. Anywhere else on your body is the jurisdiction of your superiors.'

'What do you mean, elsewhere on my body?'

I waited, my shoulder bared, my head bowed. I was so into the role now. I knew how to stand, even how to speak, if we were allowed to speak. Most of all I knew how to act meek.

'Your bottom, Sister.' I felt her breath on my shoulder. 'Because it's too close to your vagina and all those areas of pleasure.'

I slowly lifted up my nightgown. 'You mean here, Sister?'

There was a pause. I lifted the nightgown right up over my butt, and leaned on the bed to push it out at her. Still no response. I wriggled my bottom at her, running my fingers over my buttocks to open them, and suddenly I felt her take my shoulders and push me face down on the pillow.

'I'm only teasing you!' I squealed. 'I didn't mean you to be so rough!'

'You think that was rough? Oh, I think that's exactly what you need, Sister,' she snarled. 'And I'm going to show you exactly how it's done.'

I glanced round. She was holding the red scarf I'd left behind when I first came here, and with one deft movement she tied both my wrists to the bed. She pushed my face down again into the pillow so I could hardly breathe.

124

'You've sinned, haven't you, Sister?'

I nodded frantically. The pillow pushed further into my mouth. Here was someone far more dominating than me. And now she was sitting on me. The scarf pulled tighter round my wrists. I really couldn't get away. Panic coiled inside me, but so did a new, sick excitement as the scarf rasped against my bones.

'And Father Luca was too soft, or too smitten, to give you a penance. So this is just a taster.'

I twisted about, trying to get my nose sideways out of the pillow, and out of the corner of my eye I saw Sister Antonia raise her arm, palm flat, above her head. I couldn't have made a sound even if I'd wanted to. I opened my mouth, but my breath was hot and damp against the pillow. Then Sister Antonia's hand came down smack on my bottom, the sting instant and sharp. Even though I knew it was coming, I still jerked upwards with shock. I tried to wriggle away in protest.

'OK, Sister, I get it. You can stop now!'

I suddenly remembered the lack of a door on my cell. Despite giggling over seeing the other nuns fucking themselves with their candles, whipping themselves, getting it on with each other when I was certain they hadn't thought of it before, horror and shame were creeping through me now at the thought of them seeing me like this, smothered face down on the bed, my white bottom wobbling after her smack.

'Too late for that, bitch. Look at you. You've marched in here, taken over, shown us things we're supposed to be protected from. What do you say to that, Sister Perpetua?'

'I am sorry, Sister.'

I was twisting violently now. I needed to breathe. The sting of the smack was fading. I was getting light-headed with the lack of air and now I was distracted by something else. My stomach was pressed against the bed where Sister Antonia leaned down on me. I started thinking about the wine I'd been drinking that afternoon, the water at supper, and instantly my bladder swelled like a balloon.

'I hope it's genuine, but what are you sorry for, Sister?'

Sister Antonia stroked the spot where she had slapped me as she spoke, lightly with her fingertips as if tracing her own handprint. Her voice was soft, comforting almost. I relaxed, allowing myself to sink down into the bed, but that made my urge to pee grow.

'For fucking the gardener.'

'Yes. When you were supposed to be working. Though I must say the wine is fabulous. A rare earthly pleasure in here.' Sister Antonia continued stroking my bottom, so gently I could barely feel it. 'Only the gardener?'

The sting of the slap had gone. Surely she would let me get up now?

'OK. I had Father Luca, too. I corrupted him.'

126

'You invaded the most sacred of places and you have corrupted our wonderful priest.'

She lifted her arm again, and this time she was holding the whip, and then there was a second slap, harder, on the same spot. The stinging went deeper this time, radiated further, away from the soreness to touch other places. I twitched and groaned, unable to control my own reflexes now. I thought of Natalia being flogged in the chapel that first night, how she'd lifted her bottom begging for more, how remote and shocked I'd felt, yet how excited, sharing her responses without the actual pain, but this? This was like being another person, in another body which was being punished from some distance away, watching myself in a muffled dream, but beating like a drum over everything, my thoughts of Natalia, my desire for more punishment, now there was the nagging of my bladder made worse because Sister Antonia was pressing me heavily into the bed.

Sister Antonia stroked my poor buttock again, very lightly, and as she did so she started to rub herself up and down my leg, her crotch getting wet against my thigh. Suddenly she whipped my other buttock, and the shock and pain burst in a star shape and prodded sharply at my cunt. I could feel it opening, twitching, and my bladder pushing down too, opening me up there, the first drops waiting to rain.

Sister Antonia smacked me again with one hand,

whipped me with the other, riding up and down my leg as she did so. I writhed against the bed, my bladder bursting for release, all of it filling me with a mad desire for more and here it came, the nun smacking me hard again, her fingers so strong and hard they were leaving a print, I was sure, and now the pain didn't get a chance to fade or radiate because there were only a few seconds before she was striking the red, sore patch again with the whip, this time no stroking or soothing.

That quick, vicious whip lashing down again and again transported me into a kind of trance. I was floating somewhere up in the arched shadows of the ceiling observing what was happening below and feebly trying to get my head round it. I could see myself, Jennifer Coombs, businesswoman, Londoner, sex-mad singleton but never into punishment or anything particularly kinky, yet clear as day I was lying on this mean little bed, my body stretched out like a sacrifice. I was at the mercy of a wild-eyed nun who was riding me like a dervish, smacking me again and again because I'd been so bad.

I'd heard of people who liked to be smacked. Men, mostly. Judges, politicians. And until I saw Natalia whimpering with pleasure on the chapel floor I'd always sneered at the idea. What pleasure could there possibly be in prostrating oneself, making oneself look utterly stupid and low down and submitting to horrible pain? Why would you beg to be punished for some made-up crime, just to feed a fantasy? What pleasure could there possibly be in wanting to be hurt so much it would make you come? What was so sexy about smacking and being subjected to that kind of humiliation?

Well, now I knew. Firstly my crimes hadn't been made up. I really had transgressed, stormed the holiest of grounds, corrupting a priest and openly fucking a servant of the house in broad daylight. How was I to know about the spy holes everywhere? In fact, I wish I'd known. I'd have performed even better!

That brought me back to earth. As the whip lashed me again and my pussy squeezed tight with pure pleasure, I wondered if they had films of what they saw through the grilles, because it wasn't just me transgressing, was it? Oh, no. Now I knew what they were all like in here, I wanted to see what the others had been up to.

But how dark this pleasure was. I thought I knew it all, but how wrong I was. I'd always been in charge. I'd never been dominated, not even playfully. I'd never been tied down without being able to escape. And I had never been lashed with a whip. A couple of playful cuffs, maybe, but not this. The smouldering delight in being brought low, because I deserved it, being sat and wriggled on by a super-sexy, arrogant, bossy nun clutching a whip.

And how weird was this? Now I was smarting with the lashes, my skin no doubt striped with thin red welts, I wanted everyone to see it. Straining on the scarf bound tight round my wrists, I so got it. Being helpless, out of control like this, was liberating. I could give it all up. Being a little scared, enduring a particular kind of stinging pain, was exhilarating. Being ordered about and struck and told what to do and what to say and what to be was a cheap, nasty thrill and it released me from all the stress, the cares and woes of my life far away in London. And all the excitement was both in my mind, where colourful pictures of Natalia and the others flickered and taunted me, but also right here, between my legs, delivered by Sister Antonia, my body responding, jerking and rising every time she shouted and smacked me.

'You're not supposed to enjoy this, you know.' Sister Antonia's voice was harsh with her own excitement. She rocked faster, riding my leg and leaning close to pant into my ear.

I tilted my pelvis towards her, giving her something to ride, and it snagged against the rough blanket, scraped my clit against the bed. My pussy opened, oh God, my bladder started to open, warm drops going into the blanket, a warm patch soaking through. Everything was pushing down, waiting to flood out of me.

'Well, eat my dust because I am enjoying it, and so are you, you're about to come, you dirty bitch, and I wish I could turn round and fuck you properly!' I grunted into the pillow, my breath wheezing in my chest, astonished at the way I was speaking. Sister Antonia responded by starting to buck angrily, rubbing herself against my leg, her pussy lips spreading on my skin, everything getting wetter, and now she started slapping me wildly again as if she was a cowgirl whipping her mount.

As my clit scraped again and my bladder finally opened, my pussy squeezing to stop it then giving up completely, the relief of all that pressure made me come as I panted like a dog and that's when I heard the soft, rhythmic clapping of hands.

Sister Antonia leaned over and undid the red scarf, flipping me over on to my back and into the warm wet patch, and I wondered if she'd seen the other Sisters clustered in the doorway. God, she was strong. Her freckled face was rosy with excitement, her veil askew, her skirts up round her hips and yes, there was that full bush totally *au naturel*, dark-red and glistening with moisture.

I thought she was going to frig herself to climax but instead she stopped and stared down at me, spread-eagled like a puppet across the bed, and she ran her tongue greedily over her big soft mouth. Cool air blew from the open doorway over me, and I wondered what had made her stop in her tracks. I wondered if it was seeing my Brazilian, my near naked snatch, that was so fascinating to her. Maybe it was like a magnet to her, because she bent over me, her breath hot on my stomach, her mouth sliding wetly down towards my pussy, and then the licking

131

started. Soft, almost feathery caresses making my pussy pulse quietly and, God, here was the wet tip of her tongue flicking up my crack then smoothing itself flat over the swollen lips.

My head was spinning. Sister Antonia's veil had slipped enough for me to see the russet fuzz over her head, and it was jerking in and out between my white thighs and I felt ridiculously shy, should I stop this, compose myself, sit upright, make her stop, I didn't want her to taste my pee, was I going to come over Sister Antonia's face?

I struggled a little, but Sister Antonia growled, 'Keep still, Sister. I want to lick you.'

I moaned and strained, pressing down as her tongue lapped faster, sensations sizzling in my cunt as Sister Antonia's mouth wrapped round my entire pussy while her tongue probed, forcing its way further in like a mini dick, its own form of torture as her tongue flicked mercilessly and started to encircle my clitoris. As I flung myself about I wondered where she had learned this. Practised on the other nuns?

She might as well have applied an electric probe when she tapped at that tiny bud and, oh God, now she was sucking it again and again, the flicking of her tongue regular as a tick-tock, building up the pressure, pushing in harder as she munched me. I rocked back and forth, opening my legs still wider so that I was a proper feast for Sister Antonia whose saliva slurped on my pussy juice. I rocked faster, my cunt and lips and clit rubbing against her tongue and nose and chin, my hips bucking more wildly.

A bell rang out into the night. Whose coda was it? Was it for prayers? But that was the end of my ability to think because she was driving me to a final frenzy, her mouth and tongue lapping frantically. Here it came. I gripped the bed post, drew my hips back in a final glorious convulsion and my body drew in on itself, grew tight as I rattled the bed post and started to come, pushing into Sister Antonia's face, smearing my juices all over her, the thought of it driving me wild as I rubbed myself over her face until the climax had faded.

She hadn't quite finished though, and while I lay back, gasping for breath, she hooked her knees round mine and started to kiss me greedily, nibbling and biting at my mouth, pushing her tongue through my teeth as she snaked herself up and down against my wet cunt, and I opened my legs to draw her in against me, enjoying her recklessness, her abandon, the fact that I was her object of desire. Now she was coming too, slapping and smacking me feebly while she smeared herself against me, her helpless prisoner and lover, moving faster, bucking and writhing, cunt on cunt, until she reared up and shuddered with her own climax and fell down to lie, very still, on top of me.

* * *

I'd lost track of time. I had no idea how many mornings I'd woken up here, but this dawn awakening was different, because instead of the usual rhythmic tolling of the bell there was a strange buzzing sound in my ear. I screwed my eyes shut, determined to ignore it. But it was making the whole bed vibrate. I groped about under my pillow and found – my long-lost Blackberry. I stared at it stupidly. What did it want? Where had it been?

'Christ, who is this?' I hissed, rolling on to my stomach to try to muffle my voice.

'Who do you think it is, madam? Where the hell have *you* been, more like!'

I struggled desperately to get myself back into Jennifer Coombs mode.

'Hazel. Honey. I've been, oh God, you'll never believe it, I've been locked away and it was only meant to be for one night and now I can't get out.'

'Your friend told me you were ill, nothing serious, but that you'd call me after a couple of days. It's been five days now, Jennifer. What's going on? I've had that Signora Martelli calling saying you failed to turn up at an appointment on Murano, another supplier wanting you to sign off on an order.'

'What friend?'

'Some girl answered your phone. Luckily I've managed

to pacify Signora Martelli and the other orders are still coming in. I don't know what you've been doing over there, but –'

'Hazel, I don't know who that was, but I'm stuck in here, I don't know when or how I'm going to get out but it won't be long, I promise.'

'Stuck in where? What are you talking about? We booked you into the finest hotel in Venice. Hardly a prison, is it?

'It's not as simple as that. I'm not at the Danieli. I'm in this convent somewhere near San Marco. I met this girl and came to help her, and we swapped places, and now I can't get out.'

There was an Arctic silence. 'I am seriously worried that you are losing it, lady. What is all this convent bullshit?'

'Don't get me wrong, I'm actually enjoying it. Bit of R and R, then I'll be back to normal.' I kept my voice calm, because I could hear how crazy it all sounded and how angry Hazel was getting. 'I'm quite at home here, but I've lost all my clothes, my bag, my work stuff – I don't even know exactly where I am, which is why I can't leave just yet.'

My bed dipped as someone thumped down on it. Either it was Sister Antonia, come for some more flagellating pleasure, or I was in mega trouble. I turned over reluctantly, ready to confess all yet again, but it was

Natalia, dressed once again in a grey habit. She looked radiant, blooming, plumper, so beautiful. But extremely sombre.

I started to reach out for her, but she put her finger to her lips and handed me my jacket and boots. Of course. She must have borrowed them to get around outside. The phone had been in my jacket pocket all along. Which meant she had answered my phone and spoken to Hazel, but my iPad was still lost. Bugger it. All the complications of real life were flooding back to me.

'Well, you can get yourself out into the real world wearing sackcloth and ashes for all I care!' The phone practically burst into flames in my hand. 'Just get your sorry arse over to Murano today, lady, or the whole deal is off. And you're sacked.'

'You can't sack me, Haze. We're partners.'

'Try me.'

I stared aghast at the phone, but now there were footsteps marching down the corridor. I hid the phone under the pillow again, gesticulated at Natalia, but she shrugged, pulling me to my feet. We both stood to attention, but it was too late.

'Sister Perpetua. Sister Benedicta. You have both tested us to the limits with this extraordinary deception and misbehaviour. To be honest we are having trouble knowing what to do with you.'

Sister Antonia stood like a sergeant major with her two henchwomen Sister Agnes and Sister Frances on either side of her.

'Now that Mother Superior has found Sister Benedicta skulking in the streets outside, it is up to her to decide.'

I bowed my head and crossed my hands over my chest in true supplicant style, but the two henchwomen simply took an arm each and marched me and Natalia along the corridor, down the stairs, through the cloisters and into the chapel.

Sure enough, Mother Superior was standing on the steps of the altar, her hands folded into the sleeves of her stalker's coat where raindrops were slowly evaporating. She didn't look serene any more. She certainly didn't look like someone who might be handy with a pillar candle. She looked like the statue of some avenging angel standing at the gates of hell.

'We are holy people who thought we would overlook the deception and rejoice in having a fresh new Sister living amongst us. But in return for removing you from the trials and temptations of your sinful life and welcoming you into our convent, Sister Perpetua – or should I call you Miss Coombs? – you have steadily gone about our holy house turning everything you touch into sin and ashes. We hoped the novelty would pass, drop away like the spring rain, but here we are about to start Lent and we have lost patience with you.'

'Mother Marta!' I fell on to my knees, my novice's veil flapping awkwardly across my face. It sounded awful, now she put it in to words. Worse than being a naughty schoolgirl. 'Punish me, I beg you, but don't hurt Sister Benedicta. She went outside, yes, but in doing so she allowed me this heavenly opportunity to live with you all. It has truly been inspirational. I've tasted real peace here, as well as sinned most heinously. Sister Benedicta has been – all of you have been my guides. I've trashed my chance here, I know that, but honestly you all showed me what the holy life means.'

Mother Superior's nostrils flared as Sister Benedicta came up behind me and placed her hands on my shoulders to silence me.

'Don't compound your sin by speaking any more about it, Sister,' Mother Marta barked. 'You are the cuckoo in this nest, and as such you will be punished.'

As I struggled to think of something else that might exonerate me, I was distracted by a movement up above the altar. Some scaffolding had been erected, presumably overnight, and someone had started to remove the flaking plaster. One or two of the peeling, fading fresco figures on the ceiling had been partly restored, robes brightly coloured now, limbs and haloes filled in. And as I stared a male forearm rose above the dust sheets, bare to the elbow and holding a dripping paintbrush. And round the wrist was a livid red scar.

I glanced at Natalia, but she avoided my eye. She had retreated way inside herself. She was staring at Carlo's arm, too. She lifted her hands and started muttering silently in prayer, her face alight with a kind of heavenly glow. For the first time since I'd been incarcerated in here, my stomach contracted with the grip of real, icy fear.

The chapel door opened, and there was the swish of habits and the restrained tap of shoes on the polished flooring as the other nuns re-entered the chapel.

'You will both be lashed.'

I cleared my throat but it came out as a kind of whimper. 'Not me, Mother. I don't belong here, as you have just said yourself. I've said I'm sorry, but now I must leave. I have business to attend to. I'll be out of your hair before you know it.'

'And what about loyalty to your supposed loved one? All that slavish devotion gone, in the blink of an eye, to save your miserable skin?' Mother Marta produced a long wooden cane from the folds of her habit, far more lethal than any of our little toy whips upstairs.

'Mother, please!' I shrieked, beating at my chest. 'I don't deserve to be here! I'm like a, a canker worm amongst you, poisoning your sacred system, don't you see? Just cast me out into the darkness like you did before!'

'You mean set you free? Not a chance. We let you go

139

the last time, and look what happened then? You simply insinuated your way back in, bringing all your filthy ideas with you.' To my terrified amazement Mother Superior actually smiled, and though it was a cruel smile it transformed her. Her bloodless lips filled with colour as she drew them back over her neat white teeth. Her ballerina's cheekbones rose as she shook her head sharply. Her black eyes glowed like coal. 'You will be silent, Sister. This performance is extremely unbecoming. I thought you had more spirit in you than that.'

'Mother, please!'

She held up her hand, and I knew all was lost.

'We can punish whomever, however, and for whatever we choose. And you two have sinned beyond endurance. Now, lie down on your faces. Father Luca will do the honours.'

I didn't know whether to laugh or cry. Father Luca stepped forward, his eyes glinting with the same lust I'd seen before. I glanced again at Natalia, but her face was already alight with excitement. All around the nuns' eyes were fixed on me, smiling like their Mother Superior as they started that weird humming sound. I searched around for the more familiar ones, Antonia, Frances, Agnes, and they were all there, stretching their arms as if they all loved me.

The fear shrivelled as the humming grew louder and the incense smoke wafted around us again, and something else caught fire in me as Mother Superior stepped closer, stroking her whip. The other self that I had become in here, the one that rejected the terrified Jennifer Coombs, rejoiced at the elation that was to come. The stinging pain that was to be meted out on my protesting, quivering, sinful flesh. The dark humiliation that I knew would turn to darker pleasure. And all at the hands of my sexy, ruined priest.

I gave up. I spread my arms out to embrace everyone in the chapel as if concluding an operatic aria.

'I love you, Natalia,' I cried, flinging myself forwards on to the hard wooden floor and awaiting the first delicious lash from the long, wooden cane. 'I love you all!'

Chapter Eight

But my declarations of love didn't amount to a hill of beans, because my punishment didn't end there. When I returned to my cell a thick wooden door with a small food hatch had been attached to the hinges.

'So that you have time to ponder on your actions and your position in this convent,' Sister Antonia barked at me as she flung me inside and locked the door.

And ponder I did, with my little whip for company, and what I knew for sure was that I would never come back from any of this. I would never be the same again, even if I ever did escape. The pervading sense of enclosure and imprisonment inside these walls, the combination of peace and prayer with pity and pain, that sickening, low-down excitement when punishment was anticipated

– it was all enhanced just now by hearing the blows smacking down on Natalia's little bottom as she lay prostrate next to me on the hard wooden floor, hearing her own bestial moans of pleasure, hearing the muttering and moaning of the watching Sisters.

And so, Hazel, or whoever else is still reading this, in those hours and days of isolation I remembered what my little Natalia had said about trying to flagellate away her impure thoughts.

I started giving myself a few half-hearted slaps with the little whip while staring out at the grey haze of dawn from my little window, the sparse trees scratching in the garden and one or two spires pricking up tantalisingly beyond, but I quickly discovered a much more interesting ploy when I lay back on the floor one morning, still holding the whip, and forced my mind further than these four walls, started thinking of Zippo the gardener, his muddy fingers wrapped round the sturdy vines which presumably Natalia was tending again, his glossy black hair matted and tangled with leaves, his mouth wet with wine and greedy to suck on me, and what I wanted those hands to do to me if I was ever allowed back into the garden, and as I planned how they would push up my skirt, wrench away my clothes, open up my legs, kneel up between them while he scrabbled in his filthy trousers to get his cock out, my own fingers, still holding the whip, started pushing open my soft damp sex lips and held them open so that the thick handle of the whip could poke and prod at my secret hole, and I started thinking about Sister Antonia and her dark-red bush wet with excitement as she ground herself against me, and the sexy power she had over me, and little Natalia and her pretty breasts, and the other nuns watching through the various grilles and spy holes around the property, and what they would see on their flickering TV screens. Then I pushed the whip inside me, then further in, how brutal it felt, and before I knew it I was arching off the floor as I fucked myself with my own instrument of punishment.

After what felt like several days' starvation I was given some food on a tray, and when I lifted the lid on the soup tureen I found a smuggled note from Natalia.

Keep strong, my love, and we'll be together very soon. You've given up everything for me, I realise that now. Your life. Your freedom. But the positive from that is that we will be together, in here, for ever.

How could she possibly know that instead of warming me during those cold February days and nights, those words sent chills through my very bones?

As I read and re-read the note there was much rattling of keys and scraping back of bolts.

'Come just as you are, Sister. No time to get dressed. Mother Superior has a task for you.'

I wrapped my red scarf round my neck for warmth

and Sister Agnes and Sister Frances walked me silently through the cloisters, refusing to answer any questions about Natalia. We glided through attics, down passages, out into a secluded part of the garden far away from my greenhouse and my vines, and left me shivering in my nightgown in front of a kind of Cubist structure made entirely of glass. The moon and the purple scudding clouds, and the huge cross on top of the building, were reflected so clearly on the roof panels that it was like a mirror on to the sky. From across the city I could hear the rhythmic bass beat of drums in the distance.

Another kind of music was coming from within the studio. Some kind of opera. There was a snigger of soft laughter. I hesitated. Was I outside the walls without realising it? Had they actually set me free after all?

A voice called out. 'Come in, Sister. We're waiting for you.'

The room was huge. A painter's studio, in fact. Easels and workbenches leaned against the walls, and on the far side, under the biggest window, was an enormous sagging day bed piled high with cushions.

And on the sofa was Carlo Martelli, dressed as a highwayman in frock coat, breeches and a black velvet mask, straddled by a woman wearing a full red balldress.

'She scrubs up well, doesn't she? For a woman sworn to chastity!'

Carlo sniggered and slid his hand up the woman's leg and under the dress, lifting the heavy skirts over her bottom, showing white lace stockings sheathing smooth thighs and leading the eye up to her naked buttocks and, as she wriggled on his knee, the brief shadow of her pussy. Then he reclined against the huge pillows, lifting her slim frame easily on top of him.

The woman twisted round to glance coquettishly over her shoulder and the coquette was none other than Mother Marta. A raven-black Marie Antoinette wig tumbled down her back. Her cheeks were dusted with bright spots of blusher and her red painted lips were wet with saliva.

'How are you after your beating, Sister?'

This was all too much. I started to back out of the room.

'Oh, you can't go, Sister!' Carlo called out. 'Mother Superior wants to talk to you. Don't mind me. I'm just here to service her –'

'Service her? What are you, some kind of stud?'

'You got it, Sister! All that trouble with Natalia – sorry, Sister Benedicta. It's all been dealt with. All over. The obvious solution was to retain me right here in the convent, so now no one has to go outside for their pleasures.'

'Well, there was a lot of negotiating, but you now belong to me for the moment, and only on high days and holidays of obligation!' gasped Mother Marta, as

Carlo fanned his big hands over her bottom and started to rock her gently. 'As far as the other Sisters are concerned Carlo is only here to restore the chapel.'

Her small white buttocks parted as she moved over Carlo's groin, the dark dividing sliver of violet showing as her body opened and closed.

'That's not all he's restoring, you bitch!' My voice was shaking. I couldn't take my eyes off the way her muscular white legs held her as she swayed over Carlo's velvet crotch. 'Natalia is going to be absolutely gutted when she finds out about this!'

'And it's exactly that up-front attitude that we want to harness, Sister, if you'll just calm down.' Mother Marta's voice was breathless, husky. She kept her black eyes on me, her soft lips pouting a kiss. Her thighs softened, opening wider. 'And just remember who you're speaking to, please.'

I gave a bitter snort of laughter. 'You think I'm going to kowtow to you, after seeing this?'

'That's exactly what you're going to do. I will give you your instructions when I'm done here.'

Carlo lifted the nun off him for a moment and there was his cock, huge and stiff, standing proud from the fly of his velvet breeches, and in one clean movement she landed lightly down again, sliding straight on to it. Shock caught in my throat as Mother Marta arched her back and started to ride. There was something extremely familiar about the way they were moving together. It was so quiet. Almost graceful. Like they'd been rehearsing this for hours. Days, even. I wanted to rush off and tell Natalia about this betrayal, even though this wasn't the brutal Carlo she'd told me about. It was as if Mother Marta already had him tamed.

But the scene was red-hot nevertheless. What on earth was Mother Marta in her previous life? A lapdancer?

My legs started quivering with lust as Mother Marta fucked her stud, her body sliding over his cock as it went up into her. My body tightened up inside at the sight of them getting down to it, moving faster, right there in front of me, really jerking and bucking now, Carlo's fingers digging into Mother's buttocks to leave red marks while she did all the work, bouncing up and down on his legs, her pussy sucking him in, her false hair flying, and then those groans came, the ones I'd heard that first cold dark afternoon, his deep guttural groans interspersed with swear words.

Mother Superior remained silent as I would have expected her to, simply swaying her arms in the air above him as if dancing at a rock festival, tossing her hair, shaking her shoulders, arching her back, waiting for him to take his pleasure, and as soon as he started to come she jerked her bottom up and back and hard and fast, really expert, energetic stuff, so that she came at just the right moment and finally screamed into the operatic silence.

I needed to get back to Natalia, but I was frozen to the spot.

'Now, Sister, where were we?' Mother Superior roused herself after a few minutes, sitting up on the day bed and smoothing down her dress. She grabbed a bottle of wine and stood up, leaving Carlo sprawled and grinning on the cushions, and crossed gracefully to where a dark-green balldress was hanging up by the window. She chucked it at me then lay down again, first stroking her hand across the front of Carlo's breeches and pouring out some of the wine. 'I want you to get dressed up while we recover from that amazing fuck, because then I'm sending you out into the Carnivale!'

Anger surged through me and I marched over to where they lay sprawled, sweating and sated in their rumpled fancy dress. I noticed that the wine they were drinking was Natalia's *La Religieuse*, and the bottle had my label on it.

'How fucking dare you treat me to this charade? You're supposed to be all holy, superior, so chaste! And you, you're supposed to be Natalia's boyfriend!' I slapped my hands against my legs in exasperation.

'Oh, wind your neck in, Sister!' Carlo's arm shot out and he caught hold of me, pulling me hard so that I fell awkwardly on top of them both, all of us sinking down into the pile of cushions. 'Mother Marta here is in charge. Not you.'

'And that's why I want you to put this on.' Sister Marta reached up and yanked my nightgown off. 'And you should know by now that it's against all the rules to wear any garment from home.'

She tossed my red scarf over to the door before I could wriggle away an while Carlo held my legs down, she dropped the dark-green dress over my head, muffling me inside its rich musky folds, then whisked behind me to do up the tight laces at the back and pin up my hair. 'Aren't you pleased to be in fancy dress?'

She put her arm round my neck and held up a mirror to show me our reflections. My face was flushed, my green eyes blazing, still the English rose. Mother Marta's skin was pale and barely tinged with lust, the make-up garish and creepy, her black eyes glittering like a sultry witch. The low-cut dresses made our necks look longer and our breasts much bigger.

She chuckled before falling back on the bed, pulling me down with her and practically forcing the neck of the wine bottle into my mouth for a swig of red wine.

Now I found myself on my hands and knees, crouching over the wanton woman spread luxuriantly beneath me. The nun in her had evaporated into dust. Instead of her stern habit the red bodice was bursting at the seams to reveal her small round breasts and hard brown nipples peeping over the edge.

'I thought you deserved a little fun after your isolation.

150

Well, it wasn't me, actually, it was Sister Antonia and her acolytes. They've grown fond of you, Sister. In our few minutes of communication earlier they explained they are all desperate for you to stay but a woman like you can't be expected to give up her worldly ways over-night. And since no one should visit Venice without experiencing Carnivale, what better way to say goodbye to your old life than to go out there for one last fling?' Mother Marta tugged at the tight bodice on my dress, which was already making it difficult to breathe. 'Hence the fancy dress. You must admit it's a rather splendid outfit?'

'Yes, Mother. Thank you, Mother,' I mumbled. I couldn't seem to get my words out clearly. My head was spinning, my thoughts whirling to make sense of what she was saying. 'I would love to join in the Carnivale.'

Either she was very cunning or very stupid, but I couldn't pass up the chance to get out of here. I decided to play along in whatever little game she wanted me to play until she released me back into the wild. My body was already playing along with her, anyhow. My warm pussy was threatening to drip its sticky honey over her flat stomach.

'And in case you get lost or, heaven forfend, have any ideas about running away,' Mother Marta added, reading my mind, 'just remember that we are always watching you.'

Her nails dug into the soft flesh as she pulled my breasts towards her and brushed them across her closed eyelids. The sensation was sick, but heavenly. My limbs felt heavy and lazy, as if they were being filled with warm treacle. I couldn't move. I didn't want to move. I was slowly but surely losing it, and she could tell.

'I am your servant, Mother,' I whispered, falling against her.

'Good. So you won't mind if we investigate some of these wordly ways your Sisters seem so fascinated with.'

Mother Marta caressed the rounded flesh of my breasts with the merest touch of a butterfly, tickling with her fingertips, her eyelashes, even her false hair. I realised I was holding my breath, making the room seem as if it was filled with white light and revolving slowly round me. I let out my breath, arching my back, brazenly thrusting my tits towards her willing red mouth and thrusting my bottom into the air, but still the room went on turning as if it was one of those revolving stage sets. My eyelids blinked slowly to try to make sense of it, but my befuddled mind decided it didn't care. All my energy was centred on my body, where every nerve ending was vibrating.

There was a rush of cool breeze as Carlo lifted up the skirt of my dress.

'Still sore from that punishment I witnessed, Sister?' he gloated, stroking the crisscross of red stripes still raw on my bottom and making me flinch. But I was past caring whether he was getting a good eyeful or what he was going to do about it. In answer I just swayed my buttocks from side to side.

My nipples felt sharp and burning as Mother Marta's red lips parted and her tongue flicked out, just touching one burning nipple before flicking in again. I winced with pleasure and moaned out loud, embarrassed, frustrated, dull-witted. And wildly turned on.

Behind me, Carlo dug his big hands harder into my buttocks and now he was spreading open my cheeks. I moaned vaguely. I should be burning with humiliation, but I couldn't get away because now Mother Marta was sucking my nipple right into her greedy red mouth. Carlo opened my cheeks more roughly now, making the dividing flesh sting, and then he paused, as if for permission.

But not from me. From Mother Marta. She gave one sharp nod, her lips still clamped tightly round my nipple. The gesture reminded me weirdly of how she acted when she was, well, her other self.

Carlo prodded his knob into the warm, dark crevice inside me. He let it rest there for a moment. I wondered how he could possibly be hard again so soon. Maybe he was just playing. Either way I was past permitting or refusing. My head was fuzzy, yet my body was coiled tense and tight as a spring. I was being carried on a strange sea of ecstasy as Mother Marta massaged my breasts and fiercely sucked first one aching nipple, then the other. As I closed my eyes to hang on to the sensation I thought of Natalia. What we would do together if we could get out of here for good.

The two of us on a bed, on a beach, in a garden somewhere, kissing, touching, sucking each other's tits and finger-fucking each other, giggling quietly so no one else could hear, blushing at the daring of it, then doing it some more until it was no longer a luxury, it was an addiction. Doing this to each other all summer long.

But she was so far away just then. They all were. I didn't know how to reach any of my Sisters, let alone Hazel and the outside world. There was just me and this man and Mother Marta and, as the convent's Mother Superior sucked on my nipples, I wondered if she had done this to my Natalia, too. To all the others, to make them stay?

'This is one way of keeping her quiet, anyway.' Carlo pushed a finger roughly inside my tight ass, making me bite my tongue with shock. 'My big brother says she likes it rough.'

I gasped and struggled feebly. 'Your brother? What the hell?'

'Zippo Martelli, of course! Master Gardener and Vintner of Santa Maria Convent, and now upgraded to Master Sister-Shagger.' Carlo laughed, deep down in his throat. 'What a boy!'

154

'Nothing this girl does would surprise me,' murmured Mother Marta, 'especially now I've seen it all on the CCTV.'

Christ, it all made perfect, hideous sense. They were all linked, all related, all in this together. All it needed was Signora Martelli and Hazel to be in on it, too.

I opened my mouth to speak but only a kind of garbled rush of air came out. Now Carlo was impaling me sharply on his finger, rotating it from side to side in my asshole as it puckered and resisted until the tight little opening went loose and allowed the finger in, opening softly and wetly and making me gasp with the embarrassment and novelty and filthiness of it. Then he couldn't help himself, because he followed his finger with another, pushing them, rotating them to open me up, force that reluctant place to welcome him in, and the more it opened the more delicious and dirty it felt, and then suddenly he was nudging at it with the warm round tip of his prick, knocking me forwards with the force of it as my buttom weakly tried to repel him but in he went, pressing me harder against Mother Marta's mouth.

Carlo grunted with triumph, grasped my hips, and pushed himself in, inch by inch. Oh yes, he was hard and ready all right. Whatever potion was in that wine was obviously an aphrodisiac, as well as a hallucinogenic.

As he started to fuck my bottom, Mother Marta trailed

her fingers down to my pussy, which was clamouring with overpowering spasms of lust. She stroked my pussy lips, ran one finger down the wet crack, then, in an echo of Carlo's cock, pushed several long fingers violently up inside me.

I screeched out loud, rocking there between the two of them, and urgently I wanted to touch her too, discover what she felt like between those white thighs, maybe even hurt her, make her screech with lovely pain, and as soon as my fingertips brushed her pussy, it reacted like a second mouth, sucking greedily at my fingers.

'Yes, *cara*, yes, my lovely, that's the way,' Mother Marta breathed, lifting herself slightly, still licking my nipples, so that my fingers slipped easily inside. I wondered if the endearment was meant for someone else. Natalia. Or Sister Antonia. Or Zippo. Or Father Luca? But I didn't care. As fingers and cocks went in and out of our sighing, writhing bodies, I realised I was no longer torn between any of them. I wanted everyone, and everyone wanted me. I plunged three fingers roughly inside her, letting my thumb trail behind until it caught the little nub of her clitoris, and then, as if I'd been doing this all my life instead of just a few days, I rubbed brutally hard, making her fall back, biting her lips with pleasure and rubbing equally brutally at my clit, plunging her long fingers rapidly in and out of my cunt.

Carlo grunted, strong and almost silent behind me.

'This one's even juicier than the last one you brought in to me, Mother.'

He fucked my arse, making it clench round his cock, which was right up me now, sending dark delicious ripples up through my spine like waves crashing on the shore of my pussy, my arse gripping him in there until it hurt and yet felt fantastic and made sparks of evil pleasure dash through me.

I felt a demonic grin stretching my face as Mother Marta started to writhe and buck frantically on my fingers, just as I was writhing and bucking on her fingers and pushing myself back on to Carlo's forcing, thrusting cock.

'Ah, heavenly Christ, we're ready,' Mother Marta breathed suddenly, jerking quickly beneath me, her hot pussy frisking me into climax.

'So do it,' I gasped, shocked at the coarseness in my own voice. 'Fucking *do* me!'

The wave was there, ready to crash inside me, and my moaning seemed to trigger the other two, so that all three of us rocked and writhed and pushed and groaned, until one by one we came with total abandon, hands gripping, his cock thrusting on and on as if it would never stop, our pussies weeping, our mouths panting loudly, crying out as we collapsed in a heap of velvet and taffeta.

'You can go now, Sister Perpetua,' said Mother Marta

after a few moments, pushing me off her. 'Your little minder is here.'

There was a tap on the door. I staggered helplessly across the floor, leaving them both sprawled on the couch. My heart was beating like a caged bird, and I was seeing double.

'I'm ready, Mother.'

Natalia was standing there, white-faced, wide-eyed, trying to look calm. But when her eyes flicked over to Carlo her little hands curled into fists. She was wearing an emerald-green dress exactly the same as mine. She looked smaller, younger and more furious than I'd ever seen her.

Mother Marta pushed us to stand next to each other. Natalia flinched herself away from me. Had she seen me fucking Carlo? If so, she couldn't possibly think it was *my* idea, could she? I couldn't wait to get outside to speak to her alone, try to explain, but I felt as if I was nailed to the floor.

Mother Marta quickly tied green sequinned and feathered masks on to each of us and stood back.

'Remember, you are to bring her home.' Mother Marta waved us away. 'Think of this as a test.'

Natalia turned without a word and her feet in their little green shoes kicked at my crumpled red scarf. She paused, picked it up, and handed it to me silently.

Mother Marta shut the door in our faces.

'Natalia, darling! Let me explain. I didn't want to do it! It wasn't my idea! They made me do it!'

'You're far too strong for that old excuse. No one makes you do anything.'

She handed the scarf to me. I thought I glimpsed the glitter of tears in her eyes but then she turned and walked stiffly through the garden like an automaton, ignoring the lemon-smelling trees when they grabbed at her. It was as if she'd been drugged, too, or even hypnotised.

'You've got it all wrong. They've given me something. Something in my drink. Something really evil's going on here. Natalia! Let me explain!'

But she whisked through the gate in her ballgown and as I stumbled after her something clicked in my woozy mind. With or without her, this was my chance to escape.

Chapter Nine

On the other side of the gate there was a seething mass of humanity parading along the street outside. Easy to lose myself in this crowd, I reckoned, and then by hook or by crook I had to find my way back to the Danieli. I tried to turn against the tide, search for Natalia, but I was swept along by a solid wall of masked people. Some were gliding silently, some battered my senses with their violent revelry, banging drums, tootling tuneless trumpets, some were jerking like puppets or deathly as corpses, but all, of them, *every one*, had their heads turned stiffly to stare through sightless eyes straight at me as they paraded beside the water and over the spindly bridge.

I couldn't see Natalia anywhere.

Now I was being grabbed by invisible hands and pulled

into the swelling human tide of overwhelming noise and colour. My feet barely touched the ground as I was swept along, everyone drawn like magnets along the narrow *calle*, where they were forced to pause. I quickly hooked my red scarf over a rusty nail protruding from the wall on the corner. I needed some kind of sign to guide me back here, to claim Natalia when the time was right.

I kicked and punched but my struggles and screams were drowned in the torrent of noise as we flooded through the colonnades and straight into the glare and music and colour of San Marco, which had been turned into a kind of giant ballroom, or disco, depending which way you looked. Gypsy music clashed with hip-hop, the string quartet outside Florian did battle with a heavy-metal guitarist on the other side of the piazza. There was no escape. I twisted and turned to see who was holding me, but it was no one in particular. My captors kept changing as I was shoved headlong and caught in a sea of masked faces and sumptuously dressed bodies. The mouths that were visible stretched into grins. The arms and hands, all trailing lace, rich velvets and long black gloves like so many tentacles, reached out of the crowd to wave and finger and grab at me and pull me in.

Floodlights had been suspended from the corners of the cathedral and the Doge's Palace and they spun like glitter balls, bouncing light off the walls and windows and shops, making the kaleidoscope of masked figures already twirling like dervishes in the centre all the more confusing. I was totally out of control now. Drunk. Stoned. Hallucinating.

I realised there was no getting away from this crowd. That was when my panic changed into a kind of exhausted madness. I found my body moving of its own accord to the different strains of music competing all around me, and gave myself up to be pushed and waltzed between various masked companions. But then I was lifted right off my feet and tossed across the sea of bodies into the middle of the piazza where dancers moved round each other in Spirograph circles, moving me with them in the dance, and now gloved paws were going up my dress, pushing up between my legs, grabbing my bare pussy, still damp from earlier.

I wasn't the only one. Other women in all kinds of period costumes gyrated around me, invisible behind their masks. But another group caught my eye. They were attired vaguely like nuns but instead of sturdy black or grey serge, their habits and veils were of a floaty white and see-through material. They were like Vestal Virgins but their faces were covered like strict Arab women. Only their eyes, heavily outlined in shiny black eyeliner like Tutankhamun, were visible above their yashmaks.

They were spreading their arms, tossing their heads back with unholy manic laughter as they offered them-selves up to be touched and grabbed and fondled. As

one of them was flung like an acrobat high into the air
I noticed that her legs and feet were bare, and a gold
tattoo snaked up her ankle. Before I could register why
it was familiar, and what was the motif, someone scooped
one of my breasts out and squeezed it, then others
followed in a kind of feeding frenzy, velvet fingers poking
up into my fanny before I was passed like a tasty morsel
to the next partner, whose masked head would jerk curi-
ously like a pigeon, white gloves waggling like a magician,
and then a surge of energy rushed through me and I
brazenly pulled open my bodice, thrusting out my bare
breasts as the other women were doing.

The filthy reality of this orgy scenario was staring to
hit me. I spun round, dizzy with the opiate I'd been given,
horny as hell again, high on the intoxicating atmosphere,
dancing, flying. The drug dragged me up to an unbear-
able pitch of arousal, and I spread my arms and legs
wide open to say *Come and get me*.

Hands smothered me as I danced frenetically. A man
covered in petrol-blue peacock feathers groped my
buttocks. His fingers scrabbled up the warm crack
dividing them, jabbing into the buttonhole of my anus.
I jerked with delighted shock and curled my leg round
his to keep hold of him and maintain my balance, but
then he vanished, his finger sliding smoothly out again,
and another figure in a flashing top hat like a circus
master spun me round and rocked me from behind,

pushing his erection into the bustle of my dress and bundling my breasts into his hands. His white magician's gloves offered the ripe handfuls to the audience and one by one people started to approach, stretching out their hands coyly at first to have a feel, then squeezing or burying their heads in my cleavage, and then two small, slim men wearing cat masks wriggled up to me, clawing at one tit each, then bent their heads and drew the dark nipples between their teeth until they elongated and stung with painful pleasure.

People around me started to whoop and clap, or even more sexily to moan, murmur, even sing, as I became the centre of attention, at least in that little circle of the piazza. The two mouths sucked at me and it felt so wicked and good that spots danced before my eyes. I leant on their shoulders, thrusting my nipples further into their mouths, loving the pain, the filthiness of two men like big babies sucking me while others watched, in fact while others copied, the larger women in particular opening up their bodices and pushing men's heads into their bosoms to have a good suck.

While my tits were sucked other mouths and hands touched me, hard cocks encased in velvet and lycra and leather rubbed against me. I pushed my two cat-men easily down to their knees, falling on top and straddling them, my pussy opening stickily under my dress, my tits dangling over them where they could suck and chew like kittens.

Someone whipped my dress up over my bottom and huge hands gripped my hips from behind. Other hands parted my thighs, fiddling up and down the soft skin there, up between the sex lips which were really throbbing now and leaking pussy juice as electricity darted downwards from my tortured nipples. Finally one big thick cock nudged between my cheeks, and with no preamble shoved straight into my ready wet desperate cunt, nosing in like a battering ram, and my knees gave way with excitement. The cat-men were still biting my nipples, following the cock up inside me with their velvet fingers, making my hole big enough to accommodate anything.

Faces all around pushed up to see, glittering, eyeless, featureless masks peering and prying, turning to each other, sliding over each other's costumes, turning back to me, mouths agape with lust, elbows jostling for a turn.

My body jerked forward as the stiff cock forced its way up the centre of my body. Its hugeness filled me and started to pound into me, slowly at first then faster, the people starting to clap in time with my invisible lover's grunts and thrusts. On a small stage across the square I could see another woman lying on her back, legs splayed across the steps as a man in clinging snakeskin swiped his narrow pelvis in and out of her.

I went limp, smothering the cat-men as they nibbled on my nipples, let the urges inside me drive the orgasm closer. A scream escaped me as the man behind me slammed into me, faster and harder, lifting me off my feet. The clapping and stamping accelerated to a frenzy. I ground my nipples into the mouths of my worshippers as the cock exploded, and an answering wave of ecstasy surged inside me. I arched wildly to lock in the sensation for a moment longer, but I wasn't coming yet. I was too distracted. I wanted other men now. Other cocks.

I pushed the cat-men away. Their mouths were wet from sucking my nipples and with wild screeches other women descended on them like birds of prey, yapping and ripping off the men's tights and bending to suck on their swollen cocks. The tightness of my bodice had made me weaker than I realised. I couldn't stand up on my own, let alone turn round, and suddenly I was surrounded by the women in white, their huge eyes glittering and snapping with glee above their gauzy yashmaks. They lifted me by the arms feet and carried me through the bowing, clapping crowd towards the lagoon, and the sea air slapping at my face brought me briefly to my senses.

'No, ladies, please! Take me that way! I need to get to my hotel!' I shrieked as we turned right instead of left, along the waterside past Harry's Bar. 'I need to get away from here!'

'Oh no, Sister Perpetua! You're coming with us. Those are our orders!'

I squirmed and wriggled as they tittered but the feel

of their little hands grabbing all over me was continuing where the excitement in the piazza had left off, and I realised I was absolutely exhausted. I let them carry me further and further away until the music became muffled by distance, and after a while they set me down on to a slimy walkway edged by elegant barley-sugar pillars beside a tiny canal where a trio of empty gondolas bobbed mournfully.

One or two of the girls walked between two of the pillars up a steep ramp that led directly from the water into a kind of boathouse. And as they lifted their white skirts to step over the wet stones, I finally deciphered that their gold tattoos were of winged angels, painted to look as if they were flying up their legs. Flying up to heaven?

'Welcome to Palazzo Monica!' the leader of the group crowed. She lifted her white veil, and it was the same round-faced girl who had guided me from the Caffe Florian back to my convent to find Natalia. Except that tonight she was plastered in garish make-up, her face painted white with exaggerated red cheeks and lips.

'You remember us? The Sisters from Santa Monica? We are having our own ball, right here in the palazzo next door to our convent, and you are invited. In fact, Sister Benedicta is already here!'

I was dragged in to a vast ballroom with French windows all down one side and tables of food and drink

167

down the other. Jewel-red light bulbs splintered their seductive light through cracked glass shades and confused the endless reflections on the mirrored walls. A heady perfume lay like mist across the ceiling, and it numbed my head.

Up close I could see that the Sisters' white dresses were cut so low that their young tits were just balanced upon the whalebone of the tight bodice, the red nipples exposed and positioned like cherries on white scones. The full skirts of the dresses were slashed at intervals from the waist, so that as soon as the girls moved the material fell away from their hips, revealing the shadowy dip and cleft between their legs. They pulled me further inside the room, which was dazzling with chandeliers, frantic music and a dancing mass of more masked figures, but as soon as the door closed behind us the music stopped and the air crackled with expectancy.

The crowd parted before us. We filed into the centre. A low murmuring started up and people pressed round.

A violin tested its strings and the orchestra swung into a fast waltz, a kind of corrupted version of the real thing which was totally anarchic and abandoned rather than graceful and grounded. We were surrounded by a group of guests. Somehow, as my round-faced nun and the others were taken into a waltz hold, I managed to sidle backwards out of the group. I was shaking all over, but gradually my head was clearing. I could see properly now, and what I saw was Natalia on the far side of the room, being spun from partner to partner. People were lifting her skirts to prod at her legs and pussy, just as they had done to me out in the piazza, until one or two of them lingered there, keeping their hands under her skirt.

I tried to push through the crowd to get to her, but I was pressed back against the wall. A shaft of jealousy went through me when I saw Natalia's face break into a smile. Because the smile wasn't for me. It was for the round-faced nun who had reached her and now wound her arm protectively round her waist.

The jealousy was like a knife. Tears gagged my throat. At some unspoken signal the round-faced nun, who I thought was *my* champion, toppled backwards on to a velvet chaise longue, her legs splayed open, the white skirt slashing invitingly to reveal her nakedness to the gaggle who thronged round her. As the mad dancers twirled past, I kept losing sight of the tableau in the corner, and again I tried to push myself through the crowd. If the nun was distracted, surely now was my chance to grab Natalia and flee?

But then I saw her. My Natalia, in front of that crowd, and she was kneeling at the head of the chaise longue, holding the raised end of it to balance, and then she was lowering herself on to the round-faced nun, holding the emerald-green silk of her dress up over her hips so that everyone could get a clearer view of her white thighs on either side of the nun's face, the nun's brown hands grasping her legs, and her red tongue poking out like a little cock to start licking at my Natalia's fair little bush.

A rush of nausea gripped me. I knew it was useless to call out, to go to her, to do anything. It was time to think of myself.

I slipped along the wall and out through one of the French windows. The balcony outside was just above the little nodding row of gondolas, disturbed by some faraway wash and corralled like wild horses. With one last glance back into the frenzied room behind me I clambered over the balustrade and jumped down on to the slimy narrow walkway beneath, slipping over in an undignified heap.

'Eh, *signora*, let me help you!'

A man stepped out from the shadows to help me up. I shook my head, got up and promptly slipped over again on the wet stones. It was impossible to get away from here, even with bare feet.

I glanced up at the brightly lit windows, silhouettes jerking like marionettes behind the steamed-up glass. No one had come outside. No one had noticed I was missing. An idea came to me.

'Can you take me to the Danieli Hotel?' I asked the man.

To my surprise he nodded and pulled me on to the

nearest of the gondolas. I thought he would just grab the pole and we would push off in this one, but it tilted violently as he stepped through and over it, along to the next one, and I followed him to the furthest one, which had a sinister dark prow and curtained canopy. He thrust me into the cushions and pushed the gondola away from the quay and, as he steered us expertly up another canal and under a series of low arched bridges, I took a good look at his rich green breeches and splendid gold-frogged jacket.

I felt a resurgence of my earlier, drugged lust, exaggerated by my relief to be free at last. I chuckled to myself. This final Venetian encounter was meant to be, because his costume matched mine. His face was painted chalk-white and as I stared at him his mouth split into a sly grin beneath an emerald-spangled mask with a long hooked nose.

I lay back at last, getting my breath after all the dancing, running and fucking. Sweat trickled between my sore, exposed breasts although cold drizzle was falling. After hardly any time at all the man let the gondola bump along the side of a canal and tied it to a post. I knew this wasn't the Danieli, because the hotel looked over the wide lagoon and we were moored up a side canal, but when he leant over me, running his hands over the rustling taffeta of my now ripped dress, I ceased to care. A few more minutes' delay would make no difference now that I was far enough away from both those crazy convents.

'So. You enjoyed Carnivale this evening?'

'Yeah. It was wild.' I closed my eyes. I was nearly asleep there on the cushions. 'It was fantastic. Crazy. This quiet, elegant city transformed into a kind of mass rave. Something to remember when I slink back to London.'

'The guy in the piazza. He didn't make you come though, did he, Sister Perpetua?'

'So? Plenty of time to find someone else who can.' My giggle choked off. 'How do you know my name – my, er, other name?'

'Everyone knows who you are by now.' His evil chuckle was like a cartoon vampire. 'You're the only woman in Venice not wearing a mask.'

There was something familiar and dastardly in his clipped, cold tones. The gondola rocked violently as he knelt between my legs, pushing my billowing skirt up. Ice replaced the treacle that had weighed down my limbs earlier. I was too frozen with shock and confusion to move even if I wanted to but, despite all that, fresh pleasure squirmed inside me.

The water slapped beneath the underside of the boat. It could almost be slapping my bare buttocks, spread open on the cushions. Presumably in Casanova's day people wore delicate lace drawers. Or perhaps Casanova's conquests came to him well prepared, *sans culottes*.

Some revellers ran over the bridge above our heads, disturbing the peace by blowing whistles like the *carabinieri*. I tried to scream but the man's mouth pressed down on mine.

'I'll make you come, Sister. Like you say, something to remember.'

The way he kissed was amazing. Tentative, but determined. Sensitive, but wholly masculine. The way his lips held still while his tongue probed – I was on fire immediately. As I reached up to touch his face his hat fell off. His head was closely, brutally shaved. Rather like my poor cropped Sisters in the convent.

'Who are you?' I whispered. He'd kissed me before, I was sure of it. The best kisser I'd ever had.

'Just one of the many you've corrupted since you came to Venice. And I had further to fall than most,' he growled, and pulled back, tugging at the tiny buttons running down the swell of his velvet fly. 'So if you really are leaving us I want to fuck you while I have the chance.'

If he meant it to sound like a threat it came out like a delicious promise. I decided to keep schtum about my suspicions and wriggled again with renewed impatient pleasure, watching him unpick each button, the tail of his blousy lacy shirt sticking through the opening, then I could see slices of bare white stomach. He grabbed my legs and hooked them over his shoulders to keep me still.

Through the slits in his green mask his glittering eyes could now see my open, wet cunt.

And then he was ready. Laughter lines grooved down either side of his rather grim mouth as the mask eyed me silently. Moonlight caught on the silvery bristles starting to push through his skin, and I was almost certain I knew who he was. The green velvet fly fell open and there was his cock, standing up tall like a candle in the moonlight. His hands in their velvet gauntlets pushed up my skirt and opened up my legs. The gondola bowed sleepily at first, then nodded into life, then with its slow, steady rocking it started to show what we were up to. Show whoever might be watching. I glanced up to the bridge and yes, the flowing tide of pageantry had slowed. A silent crowd of watchers were up there now, sequins and jewels glinting in the dazzles off the water, all of them watching my masked lover holding his stiff cock and pushing it up between my white thighs.

He thrust it slowly into me, deep and hard, pushing me under him, down into the cushions. I didn't even attempt any token resistance. I lay there, luxuriating and loose in every sense, so tired I was practically halluci-nating, I was so far away from everyone and everything, gasping for breath, light-headed with it all, doing little, saying less, letting him take me whichever way he wanted, lying back on sumptuous cushions, missionary position, a good hard cock inside me fucking and fucking in front of an audience – I had better relish all of this because tomorrow it would be gone.

'Thank you, Father,' I gasped, then any other words became screams of pleasure, the racket ricocheting off the walls all around us as my masked lover fucked me and the gondola rocked wildly and yes, he made me come. And come. And come.

Chapter Ten

Somewhere a bell began to ring. It was the coda for Sister Perpetua. For me.

I staggered out on to the wet pavement in my green rags. Above me was the looming building with the cross on the top. And in the crumbled old wall, a door was opening, and there was Natalia. She looked tired, pale and extremely solemn. We stared at each other. She was head to toe in the grey habit, even the cloak and lace-ups, and was luminous with virtue. I was barefoot and in tatters, and hysterical with fatigue. How had I fallen so low?

My voice came out in a croak. 'Oh Natalia, I'm so sorry for everything. The sooner we're out of here the better!' Then I burst into tears.

I couldn't have timed it better if I'd been a consummate actress. If I'd been Natalia, in fact. Because she ran to me and wrapped her arms round me, pulling me against her body, warming me in her grey cloak, warming me right through. I allowed her to pull me out of the wind and pressed my face against her soft cheek, closed my eyes. She licked away the salty line of tears. I turned my head and caught her lips with mine, not sure if she would kiss me or slap me, but she didn't move, so I pressed a little harder, and then we were kissing, really tenderly, our breath and my sobbing mingling in my ears, then more passionately, pushing open each other's mouths, sucking on tongues, grinding our bodies hard against each other.

'Have you any idea how much I hate you right now?' she growled furiously, pushing her hands up my tattered skirt. 'And how fucking sexy you are?'

There was nothing to protect me, no knickers, just a bare pussy still sticky with spunk from my masked lover and tangled with my own juices, and she knew it, she could feel the sticky honey and smell it, and I wanted to get my hands on her but layers and layers of clothes kept her from me.

I fell against her as she pushed her fingers into me, opening my legs for her. I thrashed frantically against her, shocked and rendered helpless with the quickness of my climax as she fucked me with her fingers right there against the door.

'You're mine now, *cara*, and I love you, but you have to understand I will always have to share you with the others.' There was a hiss in her voice I'd never heard before. My heart gave a dull thud, stalling the blood in my veins. She pulled away from me, sucking my juices off each of her white fingers.

'The others? I only want you, Natalia!'

'And you can have me, but only if you make your choice. They are all coming for you. Your friends from London, and the Sisters, too. They will fight for you, but you have to decide, right now, before they tear you apart. Think of that crowded emptiness you endure in your worldly life, and then think of those silent sins you enjoyed with us.'

I could see the white face of my priestly lover in the gondola and the way he kissed. The chapel suffused with incense and the singing sting of Mother Superior's whip on my willing buttocks. Zippo's strong hands opening me, opening our wine. My Natalia's soft pussy.

And her face waiting for my answer from the deep shadow of her cloak.

But she must have sensed the tiny warning whispering in my ear because all at once she lifted her hand in a slap and pushed me back into the boat.

* * *

And then I woke up. I was absolutely freezing. I had lost all sense of time and space. I couldn't even remember when I'd last had a full night's sleep. And when I prised open my gritty eyes I remembered I wasn't even in a proper bed. I was out in the open air, my floor the sea, my ceiling and walls the mist of another old morning.

I sat up on the velvet cushion. I didn't know whether to laugh or cry. Laugh, because the gondola was, after all, parked right outside the Danieli Hotel. Cry, because Natalia had felt so real in my dream and to be torn away from her felt like grieving. But I had to get real. I had been had by all of them, like a lamb to the slaughter. I was battered, bruised, ripped and penniless. I had to get back to some kind of normality.

Right on cue two figures appeared at the door of the Danieli Hotel like avenging angels. Hazel and Signora Martelli, positively vibrating with anger. Beside them, my packed suitcases. Signora Martelli seemed to have aged since I last saw her. She was thinner, and paler, and, well, older. She held my iPad and my phone away from her as if they were grenades. Hazel had my shoes and coat tucked under her arm.

'What, I'm not even allowed to get dressed in my own room?' I heard the petulance returning to my voice as I stood there, hands on hips, on the pavement in the freezing morning light.

But I was tired. So tired.

'You don't have a room. You haven't been seen for nearly three weeks!' Hazel stepped forward and grabbed my arm. 'If I hadn't come out here to sort out your mess this business would have gone down the tube. While you've been in cloud cuckoo land, I don't know where, some cult or fancy-dress party or orgy or something, I've been to Murano, seen the glass being blown, ordered the items, sealed the deal, while you?'

'I wasn't far away. I was at the Santa Maria Convent.'

Signora Martelli frowned. Hazel turned to her, and Signora Martelli tapped the side of her forehead.

'I'm not mad!' I shouted, realising how demented I looked in my bare feet and tattered dress. 'I'll show you! I was imprisoned there. I was a nun. I was even flogged!'

The two of them approached me warily.

'Honey, we have to go. There's a water taxi waiting,' Hazel said, her usually raucous smoker's voice deliberately lowered, as if she was talking to a frightened child. 'You'll be fine once we're back in London.'

'Oh God, I've got to get back there. I've got to get her. Look, give me five minutes. I'll show you where it is. I know the way!'

And I took off, with the two of them cantering after me. Holding my skirts up, I rushed through the piazza, where streamers, wine bottles, discarded shoes, confetti, bras, masks and sweet wrappers all floated on the green incoming *acqua alta* like flotsam and jetsam.

'The Carnivale was real, see? It was all real!' I gave a sob of relief. 'And now we have to get Natalia out of the convent.'

They didn't say a word, but puffed and panted on their heels behind me as we passed through the colonnades on the other side, past Signora Martelli's shop and down the alleyways.

And there it was. My red scarf. Hanging limp as a used condom on the rusty nail where I'd planted it, on the corner of the crumbling wall. I ran past it to bang at the little door. There was no answer.

'By the way, Signora Martelli,' I said, turning slowly to her as a thought struck me. 'How did Carlo get that livid scar on his wrist?'

Signora Martelli went white and fell against the wall. 'He put his hand through a glass bowl when he was training at the foundry. It very nearly ruined his painting career. But that was when he was a teenager.'

'He's living here now. I expect you knew that. He's painting the chapel.'

'Oh, he was taken on when there was talk of restoring it, but they abandoned the project. Some said it was haunted. Anyway, he's certainly not here now. In fact, I wish he never had anything to do with this Godforsaken place. The effect on him was devastating.'

'You're wrong! How do you think I knew about his scar? He was here yesterday, full of beans – I saw him with Mother Superior!'

'He broke my heart, Miss Coombs. He's in the Midwest of America now. He became a priest twenty years ago, and he's running a mission over there.'

I started screaming and banging again at the door. 'Natalia! Natalia! Sister Benedicta!'

I banged until my fists were bruised, begging the twigs of the dead lemon trees inside the garden to give me an answer, but nobody came.

Signora Martelli and Hazel whispered together like conspirators.

'Jennifer.' Signora Martelli glanced at Hazel, who was also looking green around the gills now. They stood on either side of me like sentries. 'There's nobody here. This place is closed. Derelict. It's been empty for more than fifty years.'

But I know I'm not mad, because as the water taxi finally backed away in a boiling froth of water from the Riva degli Schiavoni, and I stared through bleary eyes at the city and all its treasures receding like a withering flower bed, I saw her. Natalia. Gliding across a spindly bridge, not far from the convent, her head bowed, her red lips moving in prayer. She was trailing my red scarf on the ground behind her, and sliding down her cheek under the shadow of her veil was one solitary tear.

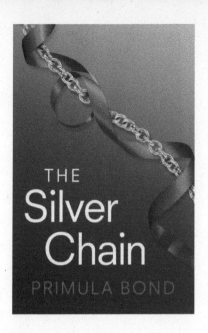

THE SILVER CHAIN – PRIMULA BOND

Good things come to those who wait…

After a chance meeting one evening, mysterious entrepreneur Gustav Levi and photographer Serena Folkes agree to a very special contract.

Gustav will launch Serena's photographic career at his gallery, but only if Serena agrees to become his companion.

mark their agreement, Gustav gives Serena a bracelet and silver chain which binds them physically and symbolically. A sign that Serena is under Gustav's power.

their passionate relationship intensifies, the silver chain pulls them closer together. But will Gustav's past tear them apart?

passionate, unforgettable erotic romance for fans of *50 Shades of Grey* and Sylvia Day's *Crossfire Trilogy*.

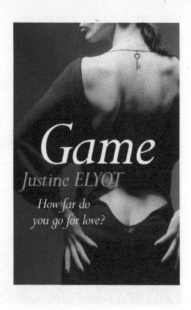

POWER PLAY – CHARLOTTE STEIN

she's the boss, everything that once seemed forbidden is possible…

Eleanor Harding, a woman who loves to be in control and who puts Anastasia Steele in the shade.

Eleanor is promoted, she loses two very important things: the heated relationship she had with her boss, and control over her own desires.

nds herself suddenly craving something very different – and office junior, Ben, like just the sort of man to fulfil her needs. He's willing to show her all of the hings she's been missing – namely, what it's like to be the one in charge.

w all Eleanor has to do is decide…is Ben calling the kinky shots, or is she?

ind out more at www.mischiefbooks.com

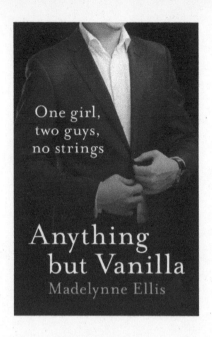

One girl,
two guys,
no strings

Anything
but Vanilla
Madelynne Ellis

ANYTHING BUT VANILLA
MADELYNNE ELLIS

One girl, two guys, no strings.

Kara North is on the run. Fleeing from her controlling fiancé and a wedding s[*]
wanted, she accepts the chance offer of refuge on Liddell Island, where she
catches the eye of the island's owner, erotic photographer Ric Liddell

But pleasure comes in more than one flavour when Zachary Blackwater, the c
ice-cream vendor also takes an interest, and wants more than just a tumble in

When Kara learns that the two men have been unlikely lovers for years, she b
obsessed with the idea of a threesome.

Soon Kara is wondering how she ever considered committing herself to just c

Find out more at www.mischiefbooks.cc